BABYLON TERMINAL

GREG F. GIFUNE

JOURNALSTONE
YOUR LINK TO ARTIST TALENT

JournalStone books may be ordered through booksellers or by contacting:

JournalStone

www.journalstone.com

ISBN: 978-1-947654-48-8 (sc)
ISBN: 978-1-947654-49-5 (ebook)

JournalStone rev. date: September 28, 2018
2nd Edition

Library of Congress Control Number: 2018949107

Printed in the United States of America

Cover Design: Zach McCain
Interior Layout: Jess Landry

Proofread by Mike Thorn

BABYLON TERMINAL

For the great Anna Kavan, imagined and actual.

PART ONE

"Woe to the bloody city! It is full of lies and
robbery; the prey departeth not."
—Nahum 3:1

CHAPTER ONE

Wearing only a flimsy nightgown, she sits at a dressing table and looks back over her shoulder at me as the surrounding darkness creeps closer. Everything is blurry and vague, as if seen through a smeared lens. Pain slams my skull, like something trapped and thrashing inside my head is fighting to get out. "Are you all right?"

The sound of her voice is swallowed by canned laughter coming from a small black-and-white television sitting atop a rickety stand in the corner. Rabbit ear antennas protrude from the top of the television, but the modest screen is fuzzy with wavy lines and crackling snow, the signal so distorted it's imperceptible. Strangely inexact sounds leak from the television, gibberish that barely sounds human filtered through odd, rumbling, machine-like noises. She turns away, but her eyes find me in the mirror over the dressing table. "Can you hear me?" she asks in a bitter tone.

Everything begins to bend and move, and the pain grows even worse.

The world liquefies, and with a thunderous roar, becomes something else.

"Can you hear me?" she asks, urgently this time. "Can you hear me?"

* * *

If you ask me how it all started, I won't answer. Not because I don't want to but because I don't know. Not really. Not totally. It simply was—suddenly—with no indication of where it began or when it might end. All I knew for sure was that Julia had gone missing.

I hesitated in the cement park and watched the skyscraper before me. The alternate version—the one in daylight—was a busy, vibrant place, or so I imagined. I had no firsthand knowledge of such things, of course, but tried to picture it alive with people, sights, sounds and smells. It was deathly quiet instead, empty and forgotten. Flags flew tattered in the darkness, reminders that this was our reality, my reality.

It made me think of a dream from long ago. I was lost, only I had left the city and was on a great stretch of sandy earth. Countless people, hidden in the jungle along the far edge of the sand, peered out at me, faces drawn. Lost as well, they stared at me listlessly, as if awaiting some promised salvation. I stood watching them, confused and unsure what to do. I couldn't see all of them, but knew there were more of them hidden deeper in the jungle. I could smell something my mind told me was an ocean, and heard what I assumed were waves crashing shore, but I'd always been told those things didn't really exist.

I'd been searching for Julia then too, but only in *my* dreams.

And then there she was, breaking through the edge of the jungle, making her way toward me with a slow and languid gait, her hair dirty and matted and draping her face, beautiful eyes hollow and saddled with black bags. Nearly nude, she smiled at me cautiously, and as I went to her, took her by her delicate shoulders and asked her where we were, she didn't answer, gazing at me instead as if she'd no idea who I was. I shook her, begged her to come back to me and not leave me alone with these *others*, these shadows I didn't know and who didn't know me. But her dead eyes looked right through me, like I wasn't there at all, and it was then that I realized I wasn't dreaming.

She was.

I pulled my coat in tight around me, crossed the cement park to the entrance of the building and slipped inside. The empty lobby smelled of a heady cleaner, and the floors still had a mirror-like glow. I moved to the bank of elevators, the revolver heavy in my coat pocket. Before I could push one of the buttons, the elevator closest to me opened. I stepped in, watched the doors slide closed. I made my floor selection.

The elevator began its ascent.

I closed my eyes and felt my heart race. In the quiet of the elevator, I felt ashamed. While mine was a necessary and perhaps even ultimately noble undertaking, the shame and fear made me want to run. But despite the rumors and wishful thinking of so many, I wasn't certain there was anywhere to run to; or that there ever had been.

The elevator dropped me off on the designated floor. I stepped out into a dimly lit hallway, the red carpeting at my feet like a river of blood coursing through a landmass of offices and cubicles. The area felt, looked and sounded lifeless, as if any trace of the living had been annihilated in the night.

I moved by a conference room, the long table unoccupied but littered, as was the floor, with papers and office supplies. In the corner a copy machine hummed quietly. I kept on until I'd reached a large glass office at the end of the hall.

"Deb," I said softly.

Slowly, a high-back leather chair behind the desk turned until its occupant was facing me. We were alone here. She, the captain of a ghost ship, manning the helm through a forgotten ocean, and me, just another body bobbing in the water—neither alive nor dead, but teetering at some point between the two.

"I figured you'd come."

I shrugged.

"What do you want from me?" she asked.

"Julia's gone missing."

"I'm aware of that."

"I need to know where I can find her."

"I've no idea."

"I don't believe you."

"I don't care."

I stepped deeper into her office, my hands still in my coat pockets. "Come on, Deb, I need your help. Julia's gone. I have to find her."

Deb raised an eyebrow. "Do you?" She leaned back in her executive chair, feigning indifference. Even now she looked ready to give a presentation—professional chic all the way in her pin-striped skirtsuit, six-inch black heels, makeup perfect, not an auburn hair out of place. Fifty if she was a day, Deb still had a body and face that turned heads, and she knew it. But none of that mattered. Not really. Deb was a shark in an ocean of fluorescent light, a killer tougher than any of her male counterparts. This was her kingdom, and she had no intention of abandoning it, whether it existed or not.

"You've got to help me," I said.

"No, actually, I don't."

"I have to find her, Deb."

"Why can't you just leave it alone?"

I looked out at the view. The wall behind her was made entirely of glass. Beyond it, a dead city waited in darkness. For what, I had no idea.

"Something happened," Deb said rather suddenly. She straightened her already neat desk and tried to busy herself.

"What are you doing?" I asked.

She shrugged, perhaps in surrender. "We all cling to what we need as best we can, don't you think?"

"Yes. Now where is she?"

"I don't know."

"Help me, Deb. Please."

She pushed her chair away from her desk enough to cross her legs. "Julia was here a few nights ago," she admitted, purposely avoiding eye contact as she scratched at her bottom lip with a bright red fingernail. "She came to me and we talked a while."

"What did you talk about?"

"She seemed fine," Deb said, rather than answer the question. "But then she suddenly froze and became strangely silent, as if she had no idea where she was or what was happening. When it looked like she might shatter into a million pieces, she began to laugh. She just kept laughing and laughing. Like a madwoman. I haven't seen or heard from her since."

"Listen to me very carefully," I told her. "There's a good chance she's running, and if so, she's in a great deal of danger."

"Yes, primarily from you."

"You have no idea what's out there, Deb."

"Look around you!" She lunged forward in her chair and slammed her palms on the desk with a loud slap. "Do you honestly think I have no idea about these things? Look at me! I'm hanging on by a thread!"

I didn't have the heart to tell her that thread had broken long ago.

Deb spun in the chair and rose to her feet. She moved to the wall of glass, her back to me. Fluorescent lights above us buzzed and blinked. They were dying too. "It's all gone to hell."

"It's never been anything but," I reminded her.

"And we'll never get it back, will we?"

"We never had it to begin with."

"Then what's the point? Tell me that."

I didn't have an answer for her, and we both knew it.

After a moment she glanced over her shoulder at me. "I honestly don't know where she is."

I didn't want to, but I believed her. "Did she say anything?"

"She kept talking about the beach, and some dream you'd told her about a long time ago, something about people hiding in the jungle." She turned back to the night, the cityscape beyond the glass. "I think it was Julia's way of telling me she was leaving the city and planning to run."

"Anything else?"

"You might want to talk to all the usual suspects," she said through a heavy sigh.

I planned to do just that.

"That's all I know," she said.

"All you know or all you can tell me?"

Deb was quiet a while. "Aren't we all in the grip of what we can never tell?"

I understood what she meant but said nothing.

"In other news fire is hot and chocolate is delicious."

There was nothing funny, but I felt myself smile a little anyway. "Is there anything I can do for you?" I asked.

"You could leave the gun."

"What gun?"

"The one you've got in your coat pocket. I need it."

"A gun is the last thing you need."

"Think I won't use it?"

"I think you just might."

"Or you could use it for me. Is that too much of me to ask of you?"

"Yes," I said. "It is."

"Leave it then. You've got others."

"I can't. I'm sorry."

"No you're not. But if you really want to make it up to me, you could stay a while."

"There's nothing here, Deb."

"*I'm* here." When she looked back this time, her eyes were filled with tears.

"I love Julia," I told her.

"So do I, but the Julia we love is gone, lover boy, *long* gone."

"I can't stay."

She wiped her eyes but fresh tears quickly replaced the old. "Was it so bad with me? Was it so horrible and ugly and foul?"

I did my best to deflect those memories…the look on her face when she came…or the way it felt when I did. But temptation crippled me. It always won, always convinced me to run to it with open arms. "No," I said, "it just wasn't real."

"It feels like I'm walking barefoot through broken glass, isn't that real?"

"We feel like that all the time, you and I."

"You think we'd be used to it by now," she said softly.

"I don't ever want to be used to it."

"Do you really think you can save her? You can't even save yourself."

She was right, of course, but if I had any chance of finding Julia, truth was the last thing I needed to believe in.

"You know that," she added, "all too well."

Eventually she softened, as I knew she would.

"Go to the ocean." Deb returned to her desk and sank slowly into her chair. "If she makes it that far, it's probably where you'll find her."

"What if there's no such thing?"

"Then you've got nothing else to lose."

I reached across her desk and gently touched her hand. I wanted to tell her everything would be all right, but we both knew that was bullshit.

"Don't," she sighed, sitting back and taking her hand with her.

"Love me or hate me, you never could decide."

"Neither could you."

Fair enough, I thought.

"I hope you find her," Deb said, voice shaking. "And I hope you don't."

I knew exactly what she meant.

CHAPTER TWO

All my gods were dead, little more than smashed idols strewn across years blurred by the very sins that had killed them. I was an assassin sent to murder myself, and I'd done my job well. The despair was unavoidable, there was no escaping it. I'd created it in place of my gods, or perhaps because of them. It no longer mattered. Their temples were in ruins and nothing could ever rebuild them. Cradled within the desolation that remained, my life had essentially become a waiting game. Waiting for the next chapter, the next bit of news, the next town, the next person...whatever they might know or choose to tell me. Everything else existed on the periphery, or as bridges between such things, hours spent anticipating the next event. It was all about being there or getting there, and even though it was slowly obliterating me, nothing else mattered. Mine was a gradual apocalypse, a slow burn creeping across a ravaged land, broken as my dreams and diseased as my memories.

I packed a bag, left my studio apartment and headed out of the city. I didn't know if I'd ever return, but I wasn't about to miss that dingy, soulless little room anyway. Nothing good had happened there. Julia and I had lived there for a time, but in a city of darkness, there was no peace in the flames, no salvation in the fire. And even when there was something akin to happiness, it arrived as a lie, a trickster dangling goodies before us only to snatch them away the moment we reached for them. It laughed at us, the night, and we laughed too, because there was nothing else to do. It had us in its clutches. What else was there to do but bleed? Sacrifices to gods long dead, that's all we were now, all we'd become.

She just kept laughing and laughing. Like a madwoman.

A starless black sky made promises it could never keep, so I ignored it and watched the mostly empty streets and vacant buildings instead. Though my battered car had seen better days, it still ran and could carry me to the deserted highways I hoped might eventually lead to Julia. But before that, I'd cover the city.

The strip was ablaze with neon lights and blinking signage, the street empty and quiet, which gave the neighborhood an eerie feel. Like a deserted carnival, everything looked open and operational, but there was no one there. Not yet. Trash and debris blew about, bouncing along gutters and across sidewalks as I crossed the street and strolled by an array of porn shops, adult clubs and the like. When I'd reached the address I'd come looking for, I stopped and lit a cigarette. The front of the building was painted to resemble a giant pair of female legs clad in fishnet stockings, spread and welcoming, the door between them a brilliant shade of pink. Above the legs, an arched and lighted sign blinked on and off in timed intervals, bathing the nearby sidewalk in intermittent splashes of neon red that read SIN-DEE'S.

As I smoked, I kept an eye on the street. Nothing. No one.

About halfway through my cigarette, I took a final pull, then flicked it away and forced myself through the front door.

I followed a tunnel-like section of hallway to a set of stairs that led down into the bowels of the building. Everything was black—the floors, the walls, even the ceiling, which left me disoriented and uncertain, but I'd been here before and knew I didn't have far to go.

Pushing through a large, heavy set of double doors, I walked into an empty club. The only light came from the backlit bar on the far wall. I negotiated my way through a sea of tables, across a series of cages positioned throughout the room and over to another side door.

As I stepped through into her cluttered little office, Lenore saw me but didn't acknowledge my presence. Instead she continued staring off into space, occasionally bringing a bottle of rum to her lips or taking a puff on a non-filtered cigarette resting on a glass ashtray on the desk to her right.

The entire place smelled of cum, booze, cigarettes and sweat.

I studied her in silence. The jet-black hair teased high and sprayed into a bouffant-gone-mad, the heavy makeup caked across sagging skin, false eyelashes batting slowly, inky appendages overshadowing sleepy blue eyes, lips painted circus-red, her aged porno-star body clad in knee-high leather boots, a miniskirt and a low-cut, skin-tight blouse.

I remembered Julia standing with me in the rain on a stormy night long ago, watching this woman through blurred windows as she moved about an apartment Julia had grown up in but had never before seen. I remembered how Julia trembled in the cold rain, even when I held her tight, and how she reached out through the darkness at the building and the woman inside who was her mother and yet wasn't her mother, as if she might somehow be able to touch her not only across such a distance, but across time and reason and the chasm that imprisoned us in this dungeon of shadows. As if by doing so she might somehow be able to better understand.

"What do you want?" she asked in a gravelly voice that sounded like she'd spent the last several hours screaming at the top of her lungs.

"Julia's gone."

She took a drag on her cigarette, her lips leaving a red smear in their wake. "So go find her," she said, exhaling through her nose.

"I intend to."

"Then what are you doing here?"

"I thought she might've stopped here on her way out."

"You thought wrong." Lenore crushed the cigarette in the ashtray, then snatched the bottle of rum and had herself a nice long swig. "But then that's nothing new for you."

"Or you."

She finally looked at me, but it was with disdain. "Why would she come here?"

"You're her mother."

"And yet I'm not." A faint trace of what may have been an ironic smile appeared, then faded. "She didn't say goodbye. But I've known for a while now she'd go. It's been obvious to everyone."

"Not to me."

"You haven't been paying attention."

"I'm going after her."

"Of course you are."

"When's the last time you saw her?"

Lenore rose to her feet. She looked shaky, but steadied herself against the desk. "You think you're gonna question me, is that it?"

"Julia could be in a great deal of danger, Lenore."

"We're all in a great deal of danger, you stupid son of a bitch. You fucking *child*. Every second of our existence is nothing but dangerous." She raised her free hand and threw it up over her head in a whirling motion, her breasts jiggling, barely contained in the skimpy top. "Look at me, what do you see?"

"I see a sad, lonely, angry old woman."

She held her ground, staring me down with contempt. "I never liked you."

"I know. Not many do."

"Can you blame them?"

"Probably not."

Lenore plopped back down into the chair, arms dangling lifelessly at her sides. She didn't bother trying to hide the track marks and bruises along her arms, and I didn't bother pretending I hadn't seen them. They were as much a part of her as her outfits and dated hairdo.

"But you love your daughter, don't you?"

She didn't answer, didn't have to.

"If you know anything, tell me. Help me find her."

"There's nothing to find. I'm all that's left." Lenore sat back in the chair, her legs sliding open enough to reveal she wasn't wearing panties.

I turned away. "Christ."

She laughed, but it soon became a rumbling cough that throttled her entire body and left her breathless and gasping for air.

I knew she'd have to fix soon, and I didn't want to be there when she did.

"Don't worry," she cackled, "the night loves her children."

I suddenly noticed a frenzied mass of flies buzzing and crawling around the ceiling's filthy dome light fixture, reminding us both of the masters that they—and we—served. Maybe they'd been there all along, or maybe Lenore had conjured them somehow, it didn't matter. The night may have loved us, but it was an abusive love, a violent and lonely love, a cold love. I watched the creatures grow in number, as if they were emerging from the fixture itself, until the entire thing became an undulating mass of flying insects.

"I'm not interested in your parlor tricks," I told her.

"We *are* parlor tricks." She smiled, her teeth stained with lipstick. "Rumors whispered in the rain…in darkness…actors performing in empty theaters."

"And Julia, what is she?"

"Gone for a reason, that's what she is."

"What did she tell you?"

"Not so much as goodbye. But I knew she'd go. I'm her mother."

"And yet you aren't."

She gripped her breasts, pushed them together into an enormous swell of cleavage. "Want me to be your mommy too?"

"Talk about a dream."

"Don't flatter yourself, *boy*. Even Julia didn't want you anymore."

"You're lying."

"Probably," she said through a heavy sigh. "Never can tell with me."

"It was a mistake for me to come here."

"Yup, sure was. Go see Joey the Creep instead, or Bobby Blades."

I nodded. "They're on the list."

It was the closest Lenore was going to come to helping me.

She slid open her middle desk drawer, pulled out her kit, a syringe, some rubber tubing, a spoon and a book of matches. "It'll be light soon, almost time to dream."

"I think Julia's going to the ocean."

Lenore gave me her best demonic grin. "There is no ocean."

Flies fell from the ceiling like ash, fluttering down across her desk and the space between us. They were dead, all of them, dead.

Giggling, she put her head back and caught some with her tongue, black snowflakes falling from a hopeless sky.

I left her there. I had no use for her illusions and depraved nightmares.

I had plenty of my own.

CHAPTER THREE

Lost in liquid static, disconnected from what I hope is reality, I see so clearly the face of my enemy. I recognize that face, and I am afraid. It knows me well, this old friend, this destroyer of light, this beast of masks and tentacles, horror and domination. No one gets away. Not really. Because its throne resides where no human can exist.

The unseen world waits…invisible…cunning…ravenous.

But all worlds are unseen. It all comes down to who is looking… and who is not.

As I fall, tumbling away from that little room I thought so safe, away from that vision of Julia sitting at the dressing table in her flimsy nightgown, it whispers its lies. There is only one way to survive what is coming, and that is through its awful embrace.

But ours is a symbiotic union. I see the symbols and secrets every- where, flooding back into my mind in a violent rush of madness. Those things right before my eyes—everyone's eyes—that we choose not to see, not to believe, bleeding evil, the crimson droplets falling as if from the infected fingertips of some ancient Rain Man.

And hidden somewhere in all this lunacy are the tricks that make me numb to the night, at least for a time, and protect me from the horrible rains of Babylon.

* * *

I'd chased him across the city and through the rain for hours, tracking him from one hellhole to the next. He was good, better than most, but he was only postponing the inevitable, and we both knew it. He ran out of time on the rooftop of an abandoned, burned out building that had once been an apartment house. The rain was still coming down hard, and we were both soaked. Some distant city lights struggling to break through the dark sky provided the only illumination, but even backed into a corner at the edge of the roof, I could see him there, squirming in the shadows like the cornered rat he was, eel-thin, with long, stringy dark hair and beady eyes.

I stopped a few feet from him and leaned forward, resting my hands on my thighs as I caught my breath. My hair was plastered to my face, my trench coat sopping wet. We'd jumped across four rooftops before reaching this one, the last in a line of rotting behemoths along the edge of a dark, bleak city.

"I don't know shit," Joey the Creep said, voice barely audible above the rain.

I straightened up, chest still heaving and lungs aching with each breath.

"For real," he said, spitting the words at me now. "I don't know where she is!"

I stared at him through the rain.

"Let me go, man." His face twisted into a helpless grimace. "Just let me go."

"Why would you fuck with me, Joey? Why would you do that?"

"I wouldn't, I—I didn't!" As he found the whites of my eyes in the darkness, he dropped to his knees and began to weep. "I was only trying to help her, man, I—I mean what the hell was I supposed to do?"

I reached for the sawed-off shotgun strapped to my leg, grabbed hold of its pistol grip and pulled it free.

"Don't," he said. "Just—*fuck*—don't! I stayed away like you told me, man, I did! I swear I did! *She* came to *me*, all right?"

"Why would she do that?"

He looked away, dripping and pathetic. "She wanted to run."

"Why?"

"I don't know, man. I didn't ask and she didn't say."

"Where was she running to?"

"The ocean, she…"

"You're a lowlife piece of shit. Why would she go to you?"

"She wanted me to run with her. She figured it'd be easier to survive if she wasn't alone and that maybe I'd want out too. I told her I couldn't do it, I—I'm no runner—you know that."

I took a step closer.

"Shit," he whimpered, bottom lip trembling. "Wait, just— me and Julia known each other forever—you know that! She came to me and I—trust me, man, I only tried to help! She wanted a weapon and she needed cash, but I—I told her I was tapped out and she should go see Bobby Blades."

"What else?"

"I let her crash at my place for the day."

"Yeah, I bet you did."

"Shit, it's—I didn't mean it like that, man."

"What did I tell you, Joey?

"I know, but—"

"*What* did I tell you?"

"If you ever found out I was around her again, you'd…"

"I'd what?"

"You'd kill me," he sobbed, his face twisted. "But, dude, listen. Please, just…just…listen…okay? I didn't run, man. You know I'd never do that, I mean, she asked but I said no. All I did was, I—I tried to help her. What was I supposed to do? She had nowhere else to go!"

"What did I tell you?" I asked again.

"Okay, I know, I—yes—but here's the thing, I don't, I mean—come on, man—why would I go to her? She came to me! I—fuck—you can't just off me, bro. I'm on the list, you—I do my part! You can't kill me!"

I leveled the shotgun and shot him in the face.

His head exploded, and in a bloody spray of rain and brain matter, his body vaulted back and away, off the edge of the roof and into the night.

With the sound of the blast still ringing in my ears, I closed my eyes and stood in the rain a while, hoping maybe it'd wash me clean. No such luck.

What no one knew was that I'd already completed my last assignment punishing those who broke the rules. I was done with all of it. I didn't care what was *supposed* to be anymore, I only knew I wanted peace. The job had left me with more demons than most of those I'd tracked down and eliminated, and now it was only a matter of time before Julia came down the pipe as an assignment. Not for me, but someone else, and I had to move before that happened. Fuck the rules. Nobody knew where the hell they came from or who had invented them anyway. I'd go after her, but I wasn't going to take her out for running. I only wanted to find her before another Dreamcatcher did. And I didn't care what I had to do to make sure that happened.

I glanced down at the blood Joey the Creep had left behind along the edge of the roof. Then I walked away, dead inside as the broken bodies and bad dreams in my wake.

* * *

Rain was still pummeling the city when I wandered into the public food district, a congested and bustling three-street neighborhood that catered to those in need of something hot, fast and easy to eat. Mixed in were cheap retail carts and makeshift storefronts hastily thrown together at the mouths of alleys or burned-out buildings nobody used anymore, or maybe never had. Pushing through the hordes of merchants, patrons, street-walkers, pimps and other lowlifes that populated the area, I made my way to a block where I often ate, then selected one of the portable food wagons that lined the narrow street. Dropping onto the only vacant stool, I leaned forward on the small counter so the awning could shield me from most of the downpour, then lit a cigarette and waited. A few minutes later, a heavyset woman in a ragged, once-ornate dress, and a colorful scarf pulled tight over black hair piled high on her head, made her way over to me. I'd eaten at this cart countless times, and there was always someone new working it.

"Let me get a chicken with beans and rice," I said above the din of rain.

"*¿Frijoles rojos o negros?*" she called back.

"*Rojos.*" I noticed the guy next to me had a bottle of beer. "*¿El frío de la cerveza?*"

"*¿Por qué no ser?*" she snapped.

"*A continuación, tirar uno de los de también.*"

Once she'd moved away, I looked around. All the merchants had awnings or makeshift sheets and tarps up, which in the steady downpour, gave the narrow street an even eerier look than usual. Mostly the same cast of characters on the street, hustling about, working the grift or looking for things they'd never find, squeezing by one another, blind mice all, hurrying off to God knew where just like always. Even the unfamiliar faces looked the same. Nothing ever really changed around here. New actors, maybe, but the same tired old roles.

Right around the time I finished my butt the woman slid a bowl in front of me, then slapped a plastic fork and a paper napkin down alongside it. The bowl held a pile of red beans, rice and pulled chicken. It was hot and there was plenty of it, although it looked somehow less than fresh. I motioned to a bottle of hot sauce behind the counter. She fetched it for me, then looked at me with an impatient smirk, awaiting payment.

I flashed my credentials, letting her know this one was on the house.

With a look of disgust I'd long become accustomed to, she stomped off to wait on the next wave of customers. I pulled my long coat in tighter around me, leaned closer to the counter, and under the minimal protection the awning provided, doused my dinner in cayenne sauce. Reminded me of blood, but then, it always had.

Somewhere behind me a woman screamed. It was loud but brief, and while some turned to see what it was all about, I powered down a mouthful of food instead. Whatever was going on was business as usual in this neck of the woods and none of my concern. I was off the clock anyway.

In a cold and unrelenting rain, I ate my meal, such as it was, and did my best to put all the horrible things knocking around in my head to sleep for a while, the lights from the carts and kiosks the only illumination in an otherwise brutally dark night.

I wasn't quite done when the stool to my left freed up. The guy eating wasn't finished yet, but when he was told to move, he moved. I understood why when I saw who'd taken his place.

Shadow was full-blooded Navajo and looked the part, from his dark chiseled features and jet-black hair hanging down past his shoulders to his wide-brimmed black felt hat, which featured a band around the base showcasing colorful tribal symbols. His coat was the same as mine, a standard-issue long trench. I couldn't remember how long we'd worked together, but he'd been in the game at least as long as I had, and that was a long time. His name was well-earned. Most runners were dead before they even knew he was there, and he had the ability to enter and leave a scene like a fucking ghost, a shadow, there one minute and gone the next.

"Been looking for you," he said in his usual monotone.

"What do you want? I'm eating."

"You know what they put in that?"

"Don't tell me," I said, scraping what was left from the bowl into my mouth.

"Mostly rodent."

I dropped the bowl and wiped my mouth. "*What* do you want?"

"Cap needs to see you."

"You running errands for him now?"

I could never tell what Shadow was thinking because, far as I knew, he only had one expression, and it was completely noncommittal. What I did know was how lethal he could be, and a sense of humor wasn't exactly at the head of his skill set.

"I was going out anyway," he finally said. "Told him I'd look around and let him know if I saw you."

I took a few gulps of beer. "So what's he want?"

"Wants you in his office. Now."

"Why?"

Shadow stared at me.

"Yeah," I mumbled, "all right."

As I finished my beer, put the bottle down on the counter and lit another cigarette, the Mexican woman returned and asked Shadow for his order. He dismissed her with a menacing sideways glance.

I watched as she gathered my trash, then disappeared.

When I turned back to Shadow, he was gone too.

CHAPTER FOUR

Neon bled through the dark, blinking and rolling and washing down from the signage and billboards scattered across the cityscape, piercing the rainfall and painting everyone in colored swaths as they slipped from one shadow to the next. It all looked so hopeless, dull and empty, and it was.

The night was alive now; people everywhere throughout the city, the crowds thicker and more aggressive the deeper into night we went. I parked in one of the designated spots, then hurried up the steps of headquarters, negotiating my way around the degenerates and homeless scattered along the way before slipping through the heavy double doors at the summit.

Dusty and dimly lit, HQ was quiet and mostly empty. Everyone was either on the street this time of night or huddled at their desks doing paperwork. I followed two long hallways and passed several offices before reaching our department, a large open room with numerous desks scattered throughout, one main office in the rear for the captain and three large windows facing the city streets below.

I crossed the room, glancing briefly at the stacks of paperwork and as yet unfinished reports covering my desk before continuing on to Cap's office.

Overweight, disheveled and pasty, he was a barrel-chested bear of a man with a snow-white horseshoe of hair ringing his bald head and a black leather eye patch, compliments of a runner that had taken his eye out with a screwdriver years before. Cap had been in the field and just another Dreamcatcher like the rest of us for years before making his way to captain, and the stories about him were legendary. No one knew if they were true because no one could remember much beyond their own lives with any real clarity—were our memories really memories? No one knew for sure—but his scars had come from somewhere.

I found him slumped over his desk, a black phone pressed to one of his cauliflower ears. He saw me and held a finger up, then pointed to one of the chairs positioned in front of his desk. A small black-and-white television on a file cabinet in the corner played an old gangster flick, the sound turned down.

Rain sprayed the windows, blurring the world outside. I sat down.

Cap was barely speaking, and when he did so it was softly, so I knew he was getting his ass chewed out. I also knew shit rolled downhill and I'd likely be next in line.

A moment or two later, he hung up the phone, dropping the handset back into the rotary cradle with deliberate care. He was doing his best to control his emotions but I knew that wouldn't last long. Never did.

"Shadow said you needed to see me ASAP."

He opened his middle desk drawer, rummaged around in it and came out with a packet of fizzy tablets. With a groan, he hoisted himself up and out of his chair and over to a water cooler to his right. "Somebody took down the Creep," he said. Water trickled into a small paper cup. "Don't suppose you'd know anything about that."

"He was running," I said, feigning indifference.

"Was he now?" Cap dropped his tablets into the water, watched them fizz. "I didn't assign you that case, did I?"

"No."

For the first time, he looked right at me with his one eye.

"No, *sir*," I said.

"Feel free to go right ahead and correct me if I'm wrong here, hotshot, but isn't that how this works? You get assigned a runner and then you go find him. That's what we do here, and how we do it, isn't it? There been some procedural changes I'm unaware of?"

"I got word from an informant on the street he was running. I checked it out, and he was already on the move, trying to put together enough supplies to get out of the city. Found him on the outskirts of Chinatown, chased him down and terminated him."

"Without authorization, let's not forget that part."

"He was running and already had a head start on me. If I waited around for authorization and paperwork and everything to get rolling, he'd have been long gone by the time—"

"Shut the fuck up." Cap gulped down the bubbling water in a single gulp. Grimacing, he said, "Seriously, just shut your mouth. I'm tired and I'm not feeling well and I don't need this shit tonight. Joey the Creep was on the goddamn payroll. You know that."

"He was a piece of shit, Cap."

"And one of our best informants."

"He was a runner."

"He was under our protection!" He slammed a meaty fist onto his desk. Everything shook. Old bastard could still throw with the best of them. "And therefore, he was on the list and not to be terminated without prior authorization!"

"Unless the Dreamcatcher in the field feels there are extenuating circumstances that necessitate immediate termination," I reminded him.

"Did you just quote me handbook, you motherfucker?"

"I made a decision. I stand by it."

Cap sat down, his old rickety chair squealing as if in pain. "How's Julia doing?"

"Fine."

"Word is you two been having some trouble."

"All due respect, sir, what's that got to do with—"

"Cut the shit, boy. You forget who you're talking to?"

I held my ground, returning his gaze with a defiant one of my own.

"Word is Julia and the Creep was old friends."

"She knew him, so what?"

"They didn't call him the Creep for nothing. Maybe you didn't like them being friends. Hell, I know I wouldn't want my old lady running around with that scumbag. What'd you do, go have a little chat with him? Things get out of hand?"

"He was running."

"Where the fuck was that moron gonna go? He could barely find his way out of a room without a flashing light over the door, and you expect me to believe he—"

"Look, that's what happened, I don't know what you want me to say."

Quiet a while, we sat there staring at each other until he finally said, "I need a full report on my desk by tomorrow night, you understand me?"

I nodded.

"Come again?"

"Yes, sir, I understand."

"Solid informants like the Creep are hard to come by. This one's not gonna go over big. I'm already taking heat for it from up above. You know what that means. We don't get this right, more heat's coming, and guess who's gonna take the brunt of it?"

I shrugged. "I was just doing my job."

"Uh-huh. I don't believe your lying ass for one minute. But you put together a report and get it on my desk and I'll back you."

"Thanks, Cap," I said, standing.

"Don't thank me. Only reason I'm backing you is because you're one of the best I've got, one of the best there's ever been." He pointed at me. "So since that's your story, you make damn sure you stick to it through thick and thin, right? I might burn when it's all said and done in this shitty world, but it's not gonna be for you, you hear me?"

"Loud and clear."

"No," he said, slamming his fist on the desk again. "I said do you *hear* me?"

"I hear you. Your voice tends to carry."

He shuffled through paperwork on his desk. "Fuck off before I change my mind."

I turned to leave.

"Go home and get some rest," he added in a softer tone. "You look like shit."

I got the hell out of there, but home was the last place I was headed.

* * *

Like blown-out speakers, the sounds of night and madness rang in my ears as I tried to sort my thoughts and ignore the heartbeat of the city. Driving through the congested streets at a snail's pace, I maneuvered through the hordes, rolling back through Lenore's neighborhood. Unlike earlier, nothing was deserted now, everything was alive and bustling and shaking with the drumbeat of the damned. A square of numerous adult bookstores and sex clubs alongside ragged but brightly lit movie marquees advertising an array of sleazy porn and exploitation flicks glided across my dingy windshield, bloody sacrifices bathing my face, multicolored phantoms feigning escape.

SIN-DEE's, rocking full-tilt boogie now, sported a line halfway around the block, but thankfully my business with Lenore was done. If things panned out, I'd never have to see the bitch again, much less be in her presence or talk with her. Images of what she and the others within those walls were up to drifted across my tired mind. I shut my eyes in the hopes it might ward off the visions. It didn't, so I drove on, eyes open and following the strip until I'd hit another intersection, this one dark and quiet. Here, only the occasional ghost stumbled along the dim streets, a pale face barely visible now and then from the mouths of dark alleys.

I stopped, watched the street a while.

Turning left would take me to the freaks, the real dark shit, the crazies that worked nightmares and the worst of the worst. The sickest degenerates and most disturbing miscreants lived down there in the deep darkness where literally anything was acceptable long as you had the juice and the desire. Evil incarnate, a carnival of sorrow and pain, lust and violence that featured every fear or phobia imaginable, it was our Hell, and a place I stayed out of unless I had no other choice.

Julia wouldn't go down there, I thought, watching the shadows slowly moving like fog, beckoning, luring me and anyone else stupid enough to entertain them down into the hole where all the forces of pure darkness awaited me. A few runners had tried hiding there before making their break, but few ever made it back out. We'd even lost some Dreamcatchers there, not killed or held captive, just lost to the madness that ruled there. I'd been to the first few streets of the neighborhood and that was enough. I could see no reason why Julia would go there, it made no sense, and much as I felt bad about outright lying to Cap, I'd already made up my mind that I was on the way out myself. If I moved through those gates and went looking for her down there, it was not only possible but probable I'd never come back.

I turned right instead, increased speed and followed the dark streets until I'd reached the outskirts of the city. Mostly old abandoned and blown-out buildings and empty lots overgrown with waist-high weeds and strewn with garbage; the area housed several rotting behemoths that no one really knew much about—giant mills and factories and the like. In fact, I'd never met anyone who remembered this neighborhood being anything other than what it was now, so no one was sure if these places had ever been alive and thriving.

Some things are born dead.

End of the night, didn't much matter.

Bobby Blade's place was a ramshackle cottage tucked away at the end of a lonely winding road. Rotting, long forgotten bungalows, most boarded up, populated the sparse lots just beyond the last of the abandoned buildings. I pulled up out front, sat in the car a few minutes and looked the place over. Hadn't been there in a few months, but bathed in the glow of headlights, with its chipped yellow paint and faded black shutters, it looked more or less the same as it always had, like the rotting carcass of a giant bumblebee. Considering the overgrown grass in the front yard and the rusty pickup on blocks in the weed-infested driveway, it didn't appear as though anyone still lived there.

But Bobby was here. Bobby was always here.

I stepped out of the car and made my way across the yard.

A dull yellow porch light came to life, cutting the darkness. I was still about twenty feet from the front door when it opened and a woman moved into view. A tattered screen door was all that separated us, but the moon was nowhere in sight and I had trouble making her out.

I stood where I was. Never could tell with Bobby, he changed girlfriends like most guys changed socks.

The moment she spoke, I knew we were strangers.

"That's good right there."

"I'm here to see Bobby," I told her.

"Who are you?"

"Bobby knows who I am."

"I asked you a question."

"And I answered it."

She kicked open the screen door and moved out onto the steps, a shotgun leveled at me. "Who are you?"

I put her at about thirty, but it was hard to tell. She'd sustained a lot of damage. Wiry brown hair styled in a mullet and bad skin didn't help. She wore old cotton shorts and a spaghetti strap tank top with a cracked decal of a kitten on it. Her feet were bare and filthy as the rest of her. "Go get him," I said evenly. "I'm in a hurry."

She didn't respond but didn't flinch either.

From behind her, inside the house, I heard Bobby say, "Easy, baby. I'd know that voice anywhere."

The woman lowered the shotgun, albeit reluctantly, then turned and went back inside. A moment later she reappeared, sans weapon, and said, "Okay, come on."

I slipped inside and followed her through a kitchen that hadn't been cleaned in months. Dirty dishes were piled high in the sink, and trash littered the floor. I did my best to ignore the smell of rotting garbage. Nothing ever changed.

Bobby was sitting on a threadbare couch in a small den decorated with yard-sale furniture and velvet paintings. The shades were drawn, and but for a few burning candles, the room was cast in darkness. He wore his typical outfit: imitation silk shirt, polyester slacks and brown huarache sandals with black socks. A razor blade earring dangled from his left ear. Blind as a mole, he had no idea how ridiculous he looked, and no one ever told him.

"Listen to you," he said through a gurgling laugh, "all badass out there talking to my special lady friend. *I'm here to see Bobby.* What's happening, baby?"

I looked around for a place to sit, decided to stand. "Need to talk."

"Cool." He reached down by his leg, retrieved a tall glass bong and set it in his lap. "Sit down and we'll give it a shake, see what falls out."

I looked to my right, where his girlfriend stood glaring at me, arms folded across her chest. I noticed she'd propped the shotgun in the corner. "I need you to give us the room."

"Go fuck yourself."

Bobby chuckled, sightless eyes hidden behind big black sunglasses. "Easy now, baby, it's just the Monk."

"He don't look like no monk to me."

"He's not a for-real monk. Ain't even his name, it's just what we call him."

"Why's that?"

"'Cuz he under the hood, baby, mysterious motherfucker, Dreamcatcher extraordinaire."

She glared at me with the level of disgust I expected.

Bobby laughed again and slapped the couch. "Known this boy forever and ever amen. We all in the shadows, but he in deep, it's how he rolls. Except for one, don't nobody *really* know the Monk. He don't allow it. Ain't that right, Monk?"

I bit my lip. "I don't have a lot of time, Bobby."

"Reba, baby," he said, smiling wide, "do me a solid and grab us some beers."

She rolled her eyes and sauntered off to the kitchen.

"What you need?" Bobby asked.

"You know why I'm here."

"Of course I know why you're here."

I pretended not to notice the pile of cocaine on the glass coffee table before him. "Then tell me what you know."

Bobby wiped his nose with the back of his hand, then reached down with the other to make sure the bowl on the bong was properly packed with weed. "You come to see the wizard. Well here I am, baby, make your wishes."

"Was Julia here?"

He hit the bong, drew the smoke deep into his lungs and held it. When he finally exhaled and coughed a cloud of smoke in my direction, he nodded. "Why you wasting time asking questions you already know the answers to?"

"When?"

"Last night."

"Anyone with her?"

"All by her lonesome, baby. Said she come from Joey the Creep's place."

Reba returned, put a beer on the table for Bobby and held another out for me. I took it, popped the cap and took a long pull. "Did she stay the night?"

An evil smile crept along Bobby's lips. "This is Julia we're talking about, ain't it? Of course she stayed the night. Her and Reba got along *real* good."

I heard Reba snicker under her breath from somewhere behind me.

"Baby, we were fucked *up!*" Bobby chuckled. "You know Julia."

Yes, I did. I also knew Bobby.

"Seeing as you weren't here—out of respect, my brother—I just watched."

"Liar," Reba muttered.

"Hey, everybody knows the rules," he added quickly. "She gonna go hugging me, them titties are getting squeezed. I'm blind, bitches, can't see what I'm doing." He held the bong out for me. When I didn't take it, he hit it again. "Next night Julia was gone with the wind, baby."

"Did she say where she was going?"

"To the ocean."

"Nothing else?"

Bobby sat statue still.

"I got to find her, Bobby."

"She's running." He put the bong on the floor, felt around the table until he located his beer. "And don't nobody run less somebody or something chasing them, you feel me? Maybe you're running too."

I shook my head even though he couldn't see me. "I'm not running."

"Well your lady is."

"Who is she running from?"

"You, baby, who you think?"

My heart sunk but I masked it best I could. "Why would she run from me?"

"You're chasing a ghost, Monk. Dig it, Bobby Blade knows all. I'm blind, but I can see. Hallelujah and praise Jesus! I can see! I can see!"

"I'm going after her."

"Business is business, right?" He licked his lips, drew a deep breath, then let it out slowly as a sigh. "You know that better than most, Monk. She's got a long way to go, big area to cross to get to the ocean."

"If it even exists," I added.

"Either way, between here and there, it's bad, baby."

"How the hell would you know? You never leave this fucking house."

"The blind man's got eyes everywhere." Bobby smiled and scratched the side of his face with his pinky nail, which was considerably longer than the others and painted bright red. Reba was smiling too. They were laughing at me, and it turned them on. "Don't nobody ever come back. Last two supposedly made it to the ocean was Matt the Cat and Frisco Sean. You remember them."

I did. They weren't assigned to me, but word was they'd gotten away.

"Like all the rest, they was gonna find the Promised Land," Bobby said, "prove us all wrong. But even if they get away from somebody like you, they ain't never coming back, so who knows?"

"Maybe they found the ocean," I suggested. "Maybe they made it."

"Maybe they didn't. Just because one of your kind didn't get them don't mean they made it."

"I don't give a shit about them. I have to get to Julia." I wanted to sit down but everything was filthy and covered with trash. "She won't make it alone, Bobby."

"Could say the same thing about any of us, even you, brother-man."

"It's not me I'm worried about. Did you give her a weapon?"

"I'm all about peace, my brother."

"Answer me."

"I didn't have no weapons to spare. Gave her what I have to give. Whole lotta love. Then I sent her on her way, dig?"

"You better not be lying to me."

"Why would I do that? Chill." Bobby leaned forward, razor blade earring swinging. "It'll be light in a few hours. You can hit the road come nightfall."

I wanted nothing more than to leave, but I didn't. I just stood there. Like always.

"Relax, we *in-a-gadda-da-vida*, baby. While they sleep, we live. While they live, we sleep."

Reba scurried into the kitchen. Seconds later the front door closed with a loud slam. When she returned, she moved from one candle to the next, blowing them out until they'd all been extinguished.

"Now we all blind," Bobby said softly.

I'd turned right on the road instead of left. Now I wondered if it really made that much difference. I closed my eyes in the dark but the Devil was still beside me, his rancid breath slowly exhaling along the back of my neck, his claws pulling me closer...*down*...into a deeper darkness all his own. *Dance with me*, he whispered, his tongue black and forked, slithering across my face like a snake.

And round and round we went.

CHAPTER FIVE

I dreamed of the light, all encompassing and washing over me like water bubbling free from a deep spring. It covered me, strangely enchanting as it was frightening, and with warm and deliberate command, slowly choked the life from me. I died in its arms, and for the first time truly understood the immensity of its power, as from somewhere beyond those blinding rays, or perhaps from within them, came the most beautiful chant-like singing I had ever heard. If there was such a place as Heaven, surely that was what it sounded like there. Like forgiveness. Like unimaginable love. It moved me to tears and allowed for something I'd rarely felt before. Hope. Strange, how little space there was between the myth of light, and the veracity of shadows.

And then Julia, screaming, not from darkness but the same blinding light, writhing and flailing about, eyes wild and hair flying. Blood poured from slashed flesh, her veins open and spilling crimson into the terrifyingly beautiful light.

Sudden thunder growled, as if from a violent machine buried deep inside my head, bringing with it bullets of acid disguised as rain, and the familiar accoutrements of night.

When quiet darkness returned, Julia was gone. Again.

But I was not. Still in the city, I had ventured to a quiet and mostly forgotten neighborhood I often escaped to when things got heavy. The area bore all the signs of having once been a central and vibrant location, though not in a very long time. Maybe it had been once, maybe it hadn't. Didn't care, really, I just knew it as a desolate sanctuary. No one ever came here, I never saw anyone come or go except for an occasional home-less person passing through. People came to the outskirts of the neighborhood but generally steered clear. They were afraid of this building, this giant structure of cement and tile, with its large wide stone steps leading up to the massive pillars on either side of the big series of doors. Chiseled into the stone above them in huge letters were the words PUBLIC LIBRARY.

I climbed the steps, the tails of my coat blowing about. A chilly wind snaked through the city, but the rain had slowed to a mist. When I reached the doors, I pulled one open, looked back out at the street below, then slipped inside.

Candles, dozens and dozens lit and left along the hallways, provided the only light. It flickered and bent and distorted along the walls and ceilings, mysterious as the wonders and secrets this monument to knowledge protected.

There was a silence here unlike any other, and a familiar musty odor filled the air. A thick blanket of dust and cobwebs covered everything—the floors, the walls, even the beautiful arched ceilings. The artwork overhead was chipped and faded but still breathtaking and unlike anything else anywhere in the city. Doorways on either side of me led to room after room of ancient and slowly decaying books. I continued on, the heels of my boots clacking against the tile floor, echoing across the large open spaces.

As I moved deeper into the building, the soft scratchy

sounds of classical music trickled down the hallway like a whisper, echoing all around me and drawing me closer. I felt a slight smile crease my lips.

Gideon. Good old Gideon.

I found her in one of the main reading areas on the second floor, in the balcony overlooking rows and rows of desks and chairs and cases of books, most in various stages of disrepair but several remaining intact. On many tables, small glass lamps were positioned at the corners, but I wasn't sure if any still worked. I studied them for a moment or two through the candlelight, and tried to imagine what it must've looked like when all those green glass hooded lamps were all alight at once.

"It was actually quite beautiful."

Gideon always could read my mind, but I'd never been sure if it was due to some magical gift or if I was just that easy.

"Gideon," I said.

She appeared from the shadows behind me, smiling fondly in the way only Gideon could. She was older—probably somewhere in her seventies—but no one knew for sure. Her silver hair was still long, but pulled back and up into a bun that rested at the rear of her head, held in place with a large platinum clip in the shape of a butterfly. Her garb never changed, an ankle-length skirt and peasant blouse, with unremarkable though sensible tan shoes.

"Shakespeare?" I asked, indicating the dusty and battered tome in her hand.

"You know all too well how intimate Old William and I have become over the years. But with intimacy comes pathos. I'm afraid he's up to his deviltry once again."

"It's good to see you, Gideon."

"It's been quite a while. Hasn't it?"

"Yes."

"Sometimes, I…I forget." She moved closer. "You look troubled." Her tired hazel eyes searched mine. "But then, you always do, child."

I motioned again to the book in her hand. "*Macbeth*?"

"*Hamlet.*"

"*To die,*" I quoted. "*To sleep...*"

"*Perchance to dream...*"

"*Ay, there's the rub. For in this sleep of death...*"

"*What dreams may come.*"

My memories of sitting here with her for hours, listening to her read to me from countless books and plays and magazines, returned to me like an old gift I'd cherished but forgotten until that very moment. Everything and anything I knew about such things I'd learned from her. I knew they were real and yet they seemed distant, like all memories, dreams barely remembered.

"And if there was one thing that fascinated old William," Gideon said, "it was, without question, sleep. *Death's counterfeit.*"

"Now that's *Macbeth.*"

"Good," she said, reaching out and tenderly placing a hand against my cheek.

I wasn't sure any of it mattered anymore, but I was glad I'd pleased her. I touched her wrist, held it a while and let her cradle my face. No one had touched me like that in a long time, with such platonic tenderness and what was probably love.

"I've missed you, Gideon."

"And I you," she said softly.

"I think about you sometimes, locked away with all these books."

She dropped her hand but her smile remained. "Do you?"

I nodded.

"What's happened?"

"Julia's gone missing," I told her.

Gideon wandered back into the shadows, which concealed a small record player on a table. She lifted the needle and the music died. That silence unlike any other returned. "Did something happen to her?" she asked.

"She's running."

Gideon emerged from the shadows, the book clutched to her chest. "And you?"

"I'm going after her."

"Are you running too?"

"I don't know. But I'm going after her. I'm leaving the city. Tonight."

"Then why are you here?"

"I don't know if I'll ever see you again."

"What else?"

"Isn't that enough?"

"Is it?"

There was no fooling Gideon, she was too smart for me, always had been.

"Is the ocean real?" I asked. "Does it really exist?"

"You remember your Shakespeare. Do you remember your Hugo?"

I wasn't sure what to say, so I stayed quiet. Candlelight danced, flickering across our faces, painting the shadows.

"*Our life dreams the Utopia*, Hugo wrote. *Our death achieves the ideal.*"

"But all these books and letters and words and stories, they belong to the others."

"They belong to *all* of us. We're one, inescapably intertwined."

"It's all a lie then, that's what you're saying?"

"Nothing is a lie, child. Not the ocean, not you, not Julia, not me, not this horrible city we're all forced to endure. It's a matter of perspective and context, do you understand?"

I slowly shook my head no.

Gideon put her book down on the table and took my hands in hers. They were cold; her skin thin and delicate, like aged paper. "It's Old William back again," she told me. "Remember your *King Lear*, the madness, the godforsaken souls. Do you remember?"

"Yes."

"*When we are born,*" she quoted in a loud whisper, "*we cry that we are come to this great stage of fools.*"

I held her hands, careful not to grip them too tight, and though I'd begun to tremble, I answered her with a quote of my own. "*Who is it that can tell me who I am?*"

"*As flies to wanton boys are we to the gods,*" she said. "*They kill us for sport.*"

"*And worse I may be yet…*"

She nodded, her eyes filling with tears.

"I'm trapped," I said.

"We're all trapped, child."

Gideon led me deeper into the shadows, beyond the table and old record player and into a back room where we'd often had coffee or tea while poring over endless stacks of books for hours. Two candles burned in sconces on the wall, giving off just enough light for us to see our way into the room. I imagined this beautiful old woman all alone in her fortress of ideas, shuffling from floor to floor, from room to room, her skirts dancing as she lit candle after candle in the darkness.

The room looked the same, a threadbare couch and chair, stacks of books piled high on the floor and scattered all about, and a coffeepot resting on a low table beneath a row of cabinets built into the wall.

She busied herself with the cabinets, leaving me in the center of the small room with my memories, visions and trembling hands. "It's cold," she said. "We could both do with something nice and warm, yes?"

"Yes." My entire body ached, the joints stiff and sore from the damp, chilly weather. "A nice strong cup of black coffee sounds good."

"Might keep the wolves at the door, if only for a time," she said.

I am the wolf, I thought, but didn't have the heart to say it.

"So you've come here hoping for answers, is that it?"

"And to say goodbye," I added.

"I likely don't have the answers you're looking for." Gideon continued preparing the coffee but looked back over her shoulder at me. "And I hate goodbyes."

"You're the wisest person I know. The wisest person I've ever known."

"Child," she said, "no one knows for sure what's out there."

I stood there like a big stupid ox, in my dirty wrinkled trench coat. "What do your books say?" I finally managed. "What do *they* tell you?"

Gideon returned to her duties. "That anything is possible."

"The ocean…"

"We've read about it in books, seen it in films and paintings, yes?"

"That's not the same."

"We know it exists for the others."

"Darkness is light here, things are different."

"Darkness is a cage, child. Light is that cage door swung open wide."

"But the light isn't our way."

"Not if we remain forever in darkness, eyes clenched shut."

"Why don't *you* run then?"

"I'm too old to run."

"Why didn't you run when you were younger?"

She offered no reply.

I thought for a moment. "Have you always been old, Gideon?"

"Long as you've known me."

"Before that, were you young?"

"I don't know."

"Was I ever a child?"

"I don't know."

"If the ocean does exist out there, what lies beyond it?"

"Does it matter?"

"Of course it matters."

Gideon turned, two cups and saucers in hand, and handed one to me. "Careful not to spill, it's very hot."

"Thank you." I took a sip. It felt good going down.

"Sit," she said, motioning to the couch. I did, and she joined me there. "There's a moment we all encounter at one point or another, a moment of abject hopelessness and primal, raw desperation. Sometimes it occurs just before death—I'm sure you've seen it in others—sometimes not, but we all experience it. When that moment arrives, when everything is stripped away and all dignity is gone, it's then that we decide if it's worth it to scratch and claw, or if we're better off letting ourselves drown in despair."

Something scratched faintly behind the floorboards. Rats, mostly likely.

"You already know what will happen if you go after her, if you run too." She sipped her coffee. "The only question left to answer is if this life is worth living without her. If you lose Julia, truly *lose* her, is there enough left to make your existence worth the nightmare it's written on? Would you rather lose it all with her by your side, or go on without her? You already know the answer. It's not me you need to ask, but yourself."

Gideon was right. She always was. Sometimes I just needed to hear her say it.

By candlelight, in haunted silence, we drank our coffee surrounded by the countless ghosts trapped within all those worn and faded pages. The trembling passed, and for the first time in a very long while, I felt quiet myself.

I knew it wouldn't last, but then what does?

Somewhere on that grand stage of fools, I imagined Old William grinning from ear to ear, up to his old deviltry yet again, just like Gideon said.

I let my mind go blank and tried not to think about anything, not all the violence and blood, not all the darkness and madness, not even Julia or what was waiting for me outside these walls.

Gideon selected a book from one of the nearby stacks, opened it and quietly began to read aloud, just like all the times before, and for a brief moment, there were only the two of us, Gideon and me, and all the wonderful memories I had of her—of us—and always would.

A boy and his mother…in an abandoned old tomb of forgotten lies…

CHAPTER SIX

Maybe I'd spent a whole day asleep, safe within the confines of that candlelit room, or maybe the whole thing had been a trick, a cruel prank born of the chemicals provided by Bobby Blade. Either way, I realized I'd come awake in my car. Night had fallen again—or it was simply later, I couldn't be sure—and I was alone on a dark and empty highway. My body was stiff and sore, and a slight headache pulsed behind my eyes in time with the beat of my heart. I opened the door and stumbled out into the breakdown lane where I'd evidently parked. The fierce rain was lost to my daydreams, but the sickness remained, and as I rounded the rear of my car, I lurched forward, doubled over and vomited onto the pavement.

After several waves of dry heaves, I fell back against the trunk and tried to catch my breath. Head back, I stared through moist eyes at the dark awning of starless sky above me and convinced myself I was all right. Like always, it would pass.

When it finally had, I grabbed my cigarettes, shook one free of the pack and lit it. The smoke seemed harsher than normal, but it helped mask the sour taste of vomit. I smoked the cigarette greedily, until there was nothing left but filter, then flicked it into the dead grass on the side of the road and lit another.

I'd had enough of the sky, so I turned my attention to the long stretch of empty road before me. Julia was out there.

Somewhere…

In the distance behind me, the vague outline of the cityscape separated from the darkness, just another shadow-dream in the land of sleep. It made me think of Deb, alone in that highrise, wandering around in her business suit and heels, clinging so desperately to addictions she could never escape; an exiled queen with useless memories frantically searching empty corridors for a crown long lost, as forgotten as the kingdom she was so sure it once represented.

It's all gone to hell, hasn't it?

I took a final angry drag on my cigarette, dropped it to the pavement and crushed it beneath the toe of my boot. As smoke trailed from my nostrils and spiraled off into the night, I slipped back behind the wheel and pulled out onto the highway.

In that moment, I'd have given anything to remember what it was like to be a child, still new to this world and all the things it had in store for me. But the memories remained elusive, as they always had, slinking away like so much smoke from my cigarettes, twisting and turning into the night without explanation or mercy. The past, much like the future, was not my own, never had been. All I had was the present.

The here. The now.

Gideon came to me, but I banished the visions of her from my mind. She couldn't help me now, and it was unfair of me to ask.

Surrounded by empty fields and increasingly untamed country, I sped up, rocketing along the highway and into the darkness before me. I watched for occasional landmarks that might let me know when I'd gone farther than I ever had before, and soon found myself in wholly unfamiliar terrain. I suppose it was a testament to how good I was at my job. No one I'd been assigned to had ever gotten beyond this point. Still, I had no idea what to expect. These were outlands, dead zones of open road and dangerous country with small pockets of residents nestled into dark little hamlets. Few ventured into these parts and even fewer ever returned from them. I thought of Matt the Cat and Frisco Sean. They'd taken off along this same highway not so long ago, so sure they'd reach the Promised Land, the ocean on the other side of the dead zone most believed existed. They'd beaten their Dreamcatcher, but that didn't mean they'd made it, or that there was anywhere to make it to. Couldn't help but wonder where they were at that very moment, though, and if they'd made it. Whatever the hell that meant.

Soon my thoughts shifted back to Julia. She was out here too. Maybe they'd all made it. Or maybe none of them had. Odds were, sooner than later, someone else would be barreling down this lonely highway looking for me.

There wasn't anyone looking yet, but once they got the idea I might be running, they'd come after me with whatever they had. Dreamcatchers rarely ran. It happened, but I'd never given any indication I'd do such a thing. Then again, it was Julia I was after this time, so all bets were off. Surely I wasn't the only one who knew that.

Night, and the highway, kept coming.

I had no way of knowing how long I'd been driving. The crystal on my wristwatch was shattered and the clock had died long ago. Strange, but I couldn't remember a time when it *had* worked. Maybe it never had. Maybe it had always been broken.

Like me, I thought. *Like all of us.*

The rhythm of the road had nearly lulled me to sleep when I saw a strange red light in the distance. At first I thought it was something in the sky, so I took my foot off the gas until the car slowed a bit. As I cruised closer, I realized I was looking at a neon sign installed atop a squat, one-story wooden building in the middle of a dirt lot.

The lighted sign read *Lumières Rouges*. Though run-down, the small bar was open, as scattered about the otherwise empty lot were a few cars in even worse shape than mine. Weary from the road, I pulled in and parked close to the entrance.

I got out of the car, went around and popped the trunk. Inside, my 12-gauge pump shotgun with a pistol grip was waiting for me in its leg holster. I strapped it to my thigh, pulled my trench coat in tight around me to mask it, then slammed closed the trunk and strode for the door to the bar.

When I glanced back over my shoulder, I saw a vision of Julia sitting in the passenger seat. I knew it wasn't real—whatever the fuck that was—but I watched her a while anyway. Unmoving and pale, her eyes stared straight ahead through the windshield at me, as if hypnotized. I stuffed my hands in my coat pockets. My left brushed the revolver, my right the shotgun.

Without looking to see if the mirage was still there, I turned and went inside.

The buzz of voices ceased the moment I stepped through the door. The handful of others in the bar remained motionless, as if some invisible switch had been thrown that left them frozen in place. I stayed where I was, just inside the entrance, and scanned the barroom. Six people total, five men. Four at the bar and one tending bar. The lone woman sat by herself at a table along the back wall, sipping a drink. Only the bartender looked me directly in the eye. A short but powerfully built older man with no neck, thick forearms and a broad chest; he ran a hand over his shaved head, wiped away the perspiration there, then cocked his head to the side like he was straining to hear something in the distance. After a beat, he offered a slow, subtle nod. I returned it and moved over to the bar. I remained standing as he wiped the counter with a dirty rag.

"Evening," I said.

The bartender offered a crooked grin.

While this was the farthest I'd ever ventured beyond the city, maybe I hadn't gone quite as far as I'd originally thought.

"What is this place?" I asked.

"A bar," he answered in a gruff voice. "What the hell does it look like?"

I stared at him until he understood I was neither intimidated by him nor interested in his wiseass cracks. "Beer," I told him.

He reacted like I'd spoken Swahili. Finally, he reached behind him to a small refrigerator beneath a wall of bottles, plucked a beer free and slapped it on the counter between us. "Only kind we got."

"That'll do fine." I scooped it up, then reached into my coat pocket and flashed my creds, flopping open the small leather case to reveal my badge.

"On the house," he said with a special hatred reserved for my kind.

I returned the badge to my pocket, making sure my coat opened far enough for him to glimpse the firepower I was packing, and then I gave him a look at a photograph of Julia. "Ever seen her before?"

"Nope," he said without looking at it.

"Try again."

"We get a lot of people in here, chief."

"No you don't. Look at it again."

With an exaggerated sigh he begrudgingly glanced at the photo—a wallet-sized headshot I'd carried on me for long as I could remember—creased and worn but clearly showing the person I was looking for. "She doesn't look familiar."

"She hasn't been here?"

"Never said that," he said through a smirk.

I grabbed a peanut from a nearby bowl and popped it in my mouth. "We can get along or I can make you sorry you ever met me, up to you."

"I'm already sorry I met you."

"You think I'm playing with you?"

"What do you want from me?"

"Has she been here or not?"

"I don't know for sure," he said, fidgeting about as he wiped the counter again.

"Tell you what. You give it some thought. Anything comes to mind before I leave—and I bet it will—you let me know. How's that sound, good?"

"Yeah," he said. "Sure."

"Then maybe I won't have to take your *fucking* eyes out of your head, huh?"

As most of the blood drained from the bartender's face, I moved away, unsure if anyone else had seen me flash the badge or photo, so I kept my eyes open as I waded through the tables toward the back of the bar. Taking up position at the table next to the lone woman in the place, I purposely waited for her to look away before I stole a glance.

Pale and powdered, with dark eyes, bright red lipstick and matching fingernails, she wore a tailored dress, light blue with black piping. Knee-length, it buttoned up the front and was offset by a thick black belt secured snugly around her tiny waist, which only further accentuated her hourglass figure. She wore black stockings and a pair of black-and-white spectator pumps. Her jet-black hair was styled in a victory roll and cascaded down to the bottom of her neck.

She shouldn't have been in a place like this—much less sitting alone—but there she was, the Black Dahlia before she went to pieces, a special order 1940s pinup girl doing her best to sip a fruity drink, bat her false eyelashes and pretend she hadn't noticed me or anyone else within a ten-mile radius.

But like me, this one rarely missed a trick. I saw it in her, and even with a cursory look, she'd seen it in me.

As the others resumed whatever conversations they'd been having when I arrived, and a buzz returned to the bar, I caught her stealing another peek. Before she could look away, I asked, "You in here a lot?"

She smiled, subtly, and broke eye contact, gazing out at the bar like there was something else of interest she wanted to see. "Is that a low-rent version of *come here often*?" she asked in a husky voice that didn't fit her.

I stared at her even though she was no longer looking at me.

I knew she could feel my eyes on her—although not in the way she was accustomed to—and I knew it was as uncomfortable for her as it was intriguing, which was exactly what I was going for. "Not exactly," I told her. "I need information."

She sipped her drink. "What kind of information?"

"I'm looking for someone, a woman."

"Most men are."

"Not like that."

"Not like what?" She gave me a quick but playful sideways glance.

I got up, took a chair at her table and sat back down, careful to keep my seat faced in the direction of the bar. "I have a professional interest," I told her, sliding the photo across the table.

When she finally got around to looking at it, she did so more vigilantly than I'd expected. "Are you a Dreamcatcher?" she asked in a far less jovial tone.

"Have you seen her?"

She pushed the photograph back to me. "Maybe…"

"*Maybe* doesn't work," I said, returning the photo to my pocket. "Is it yes, or no?"

"It's still maybe." She played with the little paper umbrella floating in her drink. "Maybe," she said quietly, "as in, *maybe* we could go somewhere and talk."

The bartender was having what appeared to be a rather intimate chat with two of the men at the bar. Huddled together, they thought they were being clever. Those types always did, and they were always mistaken. I felt the blood coursing through my temples and could already see theirs spilling.

I am the wolf.

"I've got a room around back," she told me. "Follow the path down to the tracks and you'll see the building on the other side. Second floor, first door on the right. Meet me there when…*if*… you can."

I didn't say yes, but I didn't say no. I had no way of knowing why she wanted to help me—or even if she really did—but we both knew what was coming, and soon, and she had no intention of sticking around for it. Couldn't blame her—there were times I wished I could just walk too. But things had been set in motion the moment I came through the door, and like always, nothing could stop it. Those things the lost planned in the shadows, in their own little twisted corners of darkness and fear, were irreversible. They, like all of us, were soldiers of providence, marching mindlessly into battles someone or some*thing*, somewhere along the line, had convinced us were worth fighting. Ironically enough, it was all as inescapable as the night and the damning daylight that was sure to follow.

The Dahlia pulled the last of her drink through her pretty little straw, then put the glass aside, threw me a wink and, paper umbrella in hand, slinked her way across the bar and out the door.

And then there were five.

I took a nice long swig of beer. It felt good on my throat and stopped my shakes.

The bartender and his two buddies had finished their pow-wow and were doing their best to pretend they weren't coming for me. The other two were farther down the bar and hadn't participated. They'd either leave or stay within the next minute or so, depending upon how bright they were.

As flies to wanton boys are we to the gods...

By the time I'd finished half my beer, they'd taken up position over by the front door without ever looking my way. I could tell they really didn't want any part of this. They knew what I was, and they had no reason to get involved and even less reason to get hurt. But the others had convinced them. Neither looked that bright, just a couple of rummies on break from the dreams of a drunken sailor slumped in an alley somewhere.

They kill us for sport...

One of the men still at the bar, a scruffy-looking road dog in leathers sporting a salt-and-pepper ponytail and a swagger far beyond his abilities, slid down off his stool and sauntered across the bar to a silent jukebox in the far corner.

Why did they always think things like that would save them?

"We're in the middle of nowhere," I said. "Afraid someone might hear the screams?"

Somewhere in the distance, as if in answer, I heard the sound of thunder. My own personal choir of damned angels singing to me in the night, serenading my dreams…dreams of dark addictions, the dead and dying…the running…the hopeless…

The bartender smiled but there was no humor in it. The third man, a skinny black guy with a huge Afro, was dressed in a camouflage jacket and fringed suede boots. He spun on his stool and glared at me in an effort to appear intimidating.

After starting the juke, Road Dog slid a huge hunting knife from his belt and ambled toward me with the same slow, over-confident gait he'd shown off before. As the bartender reached beneath the counter, Afro headed for me too, clenched fists at his sides. The two rummies blocked the front door.

I don't know what the hell was coming out of that jukebox, but it was loud, abrasive, violent and evil.

Closing my eyes, I reached down to the shotgun strapped to my leg, but thought about holding Julia in my arms instead—the weight of her there, so small but strong, so soft but firm—and the way she'd look into my eyes when I was inside her, like she could see something in that moment she'd never seen be-fore. Something deep inside me, another wound she'd only just then discovered. And all the while, I wanted nothing more than to tell her she was everything I wanted, everything I needed, and everything I ever wanted to be.

She slipped away, spiraling down into the dark where she belonged.

Then I opened my eyes and killed everybody in the room.

CHAPTER SEVEN

Julia wears slips even after they're no longer fashionable. And it works. On her, it works. They are elegant and sexy and real. Often, she wears a slip and nothing else, her skin glistening with a thin film of perspiration, her hair slightly mussed, a drink in her hand and an alluring smile on her face. Sometimes she wears one as we lie in bed together for hours, listening to the night die. She tells me outrageous stories she later whispers in my ear are all lies, and we laugh and make love and fall asleep just before the night burns to day. When darkness returns, so do we, stumbling about our indifferent nighttime world, vagabonds from the Land of Nod.

Though she is gone, her sadness and sedition remain, and I see her watching from the shadows in the tattered remnants of my mind. "If we knew the sun, do you think we'd miss it?" she asks. Before I can answer she tells me about a place where birds sing in flight, gentle winds blow and the air is fresh and clean. You can feel the sun as it warms you, and no one is afraid. At least not all the time.

"Fairy tales," I tell her. "Bedtime stories for the feebleminded."
"No," she insists. "It's true. They stole it from us. And we let them."
"I don't regret this life I've chosen."
Julia backs further into shadow. "You chose nothing."
I follow her to darkness, to nightmares, to the terror and screams,
and the blood that baptizes us both.

* * *

A light rain had started to fall. I staggered out the back door of the bar and leaned back beneath an overhang of roof and against the wall to catch my breath a moment. Just like Dahlia had said, a dirt path about thirty yards in the distance led to a set of ancient railroad tracks, and a small building sitting just beyond them. An old adobe structure, it was an unimaginative little two-story box with a flat roof. The walls were cracked and chipped, and though a few were intact, most of the windows were blown out. The front entrance had been reduced to a gaping hole, a doorway with splintered remnants of what had once been a heavy wooden door hanging from rusted hinges. If I hadn't known better, I would've figured the place was abandoned.

I made my way along the dirt path, crossed the tracks and into the shelter of the building. The foyer was dark and smelled musty. So much dirt and debris had blown in, it was hard to tell if I was standing on a dirt floor or one simply covered in it. A basic staircase stood to my left; three closed and battered doors to my right. Second floor, she'd said, first door on the right. Or was it the left? As I climbed the stairs I realized I still had the shotgun in my hand. I pushed back my coat and slid the weapon into its holster, just as I found myself at the top of the stairs and at the head of a long hallway. Doors on either side, all closed. It was filthy up here too, and smelled just as bad.

An overhead light blinked and buzzed, the bulb encased in a cage-like iron fixture. There was something at the far end of the hallway huddled on the floor, but in the limited and intermittent

64

light, I couldn't make out what the hell it was. Could've been a body, but it didn't look like a person. I thought for a moment I'd heard it breathing, but maybe it was just the rain. I watched it a while. It never moved, so I settled on the first door on the right and rapped it lightly with my knuckles.

The door opened almost too quickly, slightly at first, then all the way. And there she was. All pale flesh, red lipstick and hair black as coal, a white rose clipped above her right ear. She bit her lip as if she wasn't sure what to do next. "Jeepers," she finally managed. "You're covered in blood."

"It's not mine."

The dress and pumps were gone, replaced with bare feet and a knee-length silk robe adorned with red dragons. Her dark eyes dropped the length of me, then slowly crawled back up. "I don't want any trouble," she said softly.

"Little late for that, doll."

"May as well come in then," she said, stepping back and away from the door.

Inside was basically what I'd expected, a meager room with a rickety iron bed that looked like something out of an institution, a small bureau and a rolltop desk. A tiny closet with no door took up a portion of one wall and housed the dress she'd been wearing prior, alongside two others, all three draped across wire hangers. The lone window was closed, the pane so filthy it barely qualified as transparent, and the entire cramped space reeked of cigarettes, booze, perfume and pussy. Sparse light emanated from a candle burning on the bureau, leaving behind plenty of shadow.

She closed the door behind me, leaned back against it, and then, feigning modesty, pulled her robe in tighter around her.

"There any running water in this building?" I asked.

The Dahlia pointed a bright red fingernail at a small basin on the floor next to the bed. Filled with water, a washcloth was draped over its side. "There's enough there to wash up with."

I pulled off my coat, tossed it over the foot of the bed, then crouched next to the basin, grabbed the cloth and submerged it in the tepid water. It slowly turned crimson as the blood on my hands drifted free.

"Did you kill them?" she asked, just above a whisper.

She already knew the answer, and it turned her on. She was that type. I could tell. I'd seen plenty like her before, those who couldn't bear to watch such things but lived to hear about them. I peered down into the basin instead, watching the swirl of blood curling through the water.

"How did…" Her breath caught in her throat. "How did you do it?"

I squeezed out the washcloth and brought it to my face, feeling the water drip and run along my throat and down onto my chest as I cleaned the blood from my face. My ears were still ringing, and my body was sore and stiff.

"Tell me," Dahlia pleaded. "And I'll tell you what you want to know."

I pull the shotgun from my leg, level it, pump and fire then pump and fire again, blowing both Afro and Road Dog back toward the bar from which they'd come, their bodies airborne as chunks of abdomen and chest explode, spraying the floor, the walls, and me.

She didn't yet understand that she'd tell me what I wanted to know regardless.

I come up out of my chair, the shotgun in one hand and the chair in the other. Hurling the chair toward the door, I spin, pump and fire again, this time hitting the bartender as he rounds the end of the bar. He screams as the lower portion of his right leg below the knee separates from the rest of his body, flopping onto the floor in a grisly spray of bone, blood, flesh and muscle.

I ran the washcloth over my throat and then around to the back of my neck. "I'm not here to make deals," I said.

The two cretins blocking the front door avoid the chair and try to run, stumbling out the entrance fast as they can. I shoot them both as they try to escape, one in the back of his head, the other between the shoulder blades. The first dies instantly, the second flops around a while before he goes quiet. The bartender continues to scream and writhe about on the floor in a pool of his own blood, shit, piss and tears, clutching at the grotesque mangled stump that is now his leg.

"You can tell me all about it. It's okay."

"I'm here for information," I said. "And you're going to give it to me."

I shoot the jukebox so I can hear myself think, then I kneel on the bartender's chest, reach down and cup the side of his face. "Shhh," I whisper, repeating it again and again until he finally quiets down. His body continues to convulse beneath me, his eyes wild with disbelief, horror and agony. "Close your eyes now, it'll be all right."

"You didn't have to kill them, did you?" she persisted. "Your kind just likes it, huh? You like it, right? You like the violence, the kill."

"Is there anything to drink in here?" I asked.

"I don't have any beer if that's what—"

"Something harder," I said.

She motioned with her chin to the bureau. There was a small bottle of vodka there.

As the bartender closes his eyes, I lay the shotgun on the floor and cup his face again, this time with both hands, my thumbs under his eyes. Slowly, I slide them higher and press them into his sockets. He groans, and I lean closer, close enough so I can whisper in his ear and tell him more lies. Then I press my thumbs into his eyes, popping and exploding them in the sockets as he grips my wrists, gags and cries out. I push deeper and impossibly deeper still…until the crying stops…until the convulsing stops. And then he is quiet and still, our dance is over, and I am alone with the dead.

Rain sprayed the window. I tossed the cloth into the basin and rose to my feet. "The woman in the photograph," I said, moving toward the bureau. "She was here?"

The Dahlia nodded. "Last night."

I was still a day behind her. "Was she alone?"

She nodded again.

"Did you talk to her?"

"A little, but she mostly talked to Rodney. That's the guy who was tending bar."

"What'd they talk about?"

"I don't listen in on other peoples' conversations."

"Sure you do. What'd they talk about?"

The Dahlia frowned. "She said she needed help, said she was running. She told Rodney she needed a weapon."

"And did he oblige?"

"Huh?"

With a sigh, I grabbed the bottle from the bureau. "Did he give her a weapon?"

"Oh. Yeah, he gave her a pistol. Not sure what kind. I dunno much about guns."

"And what'd she give him?"

She smirked but remained leaned against the door. "Three guesses and the first two don't count."

That explained the attack. Once you got close to her, once you felt like you knew her, you wanted to be a hero for her, to help her, to save her. Julia. Goddamn Julia.

"Odd question for a Dreamcatcher to ask," she said. "You know her, huh?"

I spun the cap and threw back a long pull of vodka. The burn felt good. Wiping my mouth with the back of my hand, I walked around to the foot of the bed and sat down next to my coat. "She's my wife."

"Sweet Georgia Brown! Your own wife's a runner?" The Dahlia slapped her bare thigh. "And *you're* chasing her?"

I unstrapped the holster from my thigh and tossed it, along with the shotgun, onto the bed. "Just trying to find her and bring her home is all."

"Doesn't much sound to me like home is a place she wants to be." She delicately traced her circus lips with the tip of her tongue. "Why'd she run?"

"Why's anybody run?"

"So it's not business then, strictly personal, huh? Or maybe you're running too."

Rather than answer, I took another swig of vodka.

"She looked scared. I felt bad for her. It's tough for a gal all alone out here." She twirled her hair with a fingertip. "It's tough for a gal all alone everywhere."

"Have you been farther out than this?" I asked.

"Not much. Those are the outlands. Crazies out there worse than anything we got here or in the city, that's nightmare land."

"And Julia's headed right for it."

"So are you." She finally pushed away from the door and came closer, but slowly, cautiously. "They say there's an ocean on the other side…and beyond that…the Promised Land."

"You believe in that?"

"I don't know. I've never seen a for-real ocean. Do you believe it?"

I held the bottle out for her.

She took it, and once she'd figured out I had no intention of answering her, said, "It'll be light soon. Do you want to stay? You look like you could use some sleep, and we could"—she wiped the bottle with the sleeve of her robe before bringing it to her lips—"maybe…get to know each other better."

"Don't you have anything else to do?"

"Not a lot of work for me these days. I'm kind of a specialty, you know?"

"An acquired taste," I said.

"Just like you." She took another sip, then smiled at me with bright, beautiful teeth. "What's your name, anyway?"

"They call me Monk."

"*Monk?*" She arched an eyebrow. "Gee, mister, that's kinda creepy."

I laughed, albeit lightly. Couldn't remember the last time that had happened.

"Lucky for me," I said, "so are you."

She became oddly silent, and the flirting routine receded. "I saw a Dreamcatcher once before, but I've never actually talked to one. It's a little scary."

"I'm thinking you don't scare too easy."

"I'm not a tough girl."

"You're tough enough."

"I'm lonely," she said, then looked away as if the words had escaped without her permission. "I ride out the nights here."

"Why here?"

The Dahlia shrugged. "Nowhere else to go, and I'm not cut out to run."

"Could always take over the bar," I said. "It's just become available."

A coy smile returned to her face. "Maybe I will."

I unbuttoned my shirt, pulled it off my shoulders and tossed it aside. It was specked with sprays of blood. Her eyes immediately went to the long scar on my chest, which began under my throat and arced across my pectoral muscle nearly to my navel. A little souvenir a runner had given me in an alley a long time ago—exactly when I couldn't recall, like all memories, they were sketchy and vague—but I remembered the broken bottle he'd used to cut me, slashing it at me out of the shadows like a knife. I also remembered tearing out his throat while he was still alive, then watching him die in that alley while I bled all over him. The others were scattered across my abdomen, back, shoulders and arms, two ugly scars from bullet wounds, the rest from knives or whatever else runners could get their hands on when they were cornered. Every one of them was a reminder to me that every assignment could be my last, and that if I'd done my job properly, they'd have never had the chance to do me any harm.

The Dahlia handed the bottle back, her hand shaking.

I downed another gulp of vodka, maybe two, as her eyes glided back and forth between all the mayhem on my flesh and the numerous black tribal tattoos I had emblazoned nearly everywhere else.

"You're not gonna hurt me, are you?" she asked.

I felt myself drifting away, lost in the booze, my exhaustion and her sadly tragic beauty. "Do you want me to hurt you?"

She slowly slipped off the robe and let it fall to the floor. Standing naked before me, several scars of her own littered her otherwise pale, porcelain-like skin. Blood-red lips trembling, she ran a hand up her long white neck, around to the back of her head and pulled loose her hair. It cascaded down to her shoulders in dark waves as she cupped her breasts and cocked her head to the side. The rose fell free, spiraling to the floor like a broken promise. It had turned brittle and black, rotten. "What do you think?"

There was no remedy, only the coming dawn.

And just like that, the Devil was back, talons clicking on the window and disguised as God's rain.

CHAPTER EIGHT

The light burned away, day turned to dusk, and night finally fell. Life, or something similar, returned to me, filling my body and mind like a rush of oxygen fed directly into my lungs. Returned to darkness, home in my labyrinth of dreams, the world was a rumor no more.

The Dahlia was already awake, lying there next to me, her falsely innocent eyes batting at me. "You were talking in your sleep," she said. "Sounded scared—terrified—like something was chasing *you*. I guess even a Dreamcatcher has nightmares, huh?"

You have no idea. I pawed at my eyes and tried to move, suddenly aware of every ache and pain and injury my body had ever endured. Reaching down to the floor, I located my weapons, as they'd been knocked from the bed earlier. They'd become as much a part of me as my eyes, hands or legs, my heart.

"When you leave…" she said, delicately dragging a fingernail through the tuft of hair on my chest, "can I come with you?"

"Can't let you do that."

"You mean you won't."

I slid out from beneath her, swung my feet to the floor and sat up. Night bled through the window. "You don't want to go where I'm headed. It's no place for you."

"And this is?"

As I forced myself to my feet and reached for my clothes, she scooted up into a sitting position, bringing the sheet with her. I found my cigarettes on the nightstand, placed two between my lips, lit them both, then handed one to her. "Go somewhere else," I said. "Where are you from?"

Baffled by my question, she was quiet a moment. "I don't know," she finally admitted. "I...I'm not sure, really. Here, I guess. I have memories, but...they all seem so far away. Sometimes it's almost like they're not even really mine. I'm just...here. It's kinda like when we work, you know? It just...happens. You're there and doing your thing but you're not really sure how or why. Then it's over and hard to remember."

"Go to the city," I suggested.

"I hear it's dying."

"Everything's dying."

"Even us?"

We can only hope, I thought.

"Do you remember being a child?" she asked rather abruptly.

Strange flashes of what might have been childhood memories blinked across my mind's eye—*a beautiful field where a little boy played with his puppy, blurry visions of my home*—but they were so disjointed and surreal I couldn't get a useful or meaningful read on them.

"Not really," I said, stepping into my pants.

"Me neither. Why do you think that is?"

My shirt was stained with blood, but it was the only one I had, so I slipped into it and then pulled on my boots. "You ask a lot of questions."

"Do you think it's because...maybe...we were never really children at all?"

I scratched at the stubble along my jaw. The same shrieking demons from my nightmares were still gnawing on my bones, safely hidden in the land of sleep, their war cry echoing in my head. Or perhaps the screams were my own. Who could be sure?

The Dahlia smoked her cigarette and looked away, apparently mulling over her question. "They say that's where the children are, you know, in the outlands. They say that's where they live. I mean, I've worked with kids a few times, but other than that, you never see them."

"I don't deal with children. They don't run."

"Maybe they don't know any better."

Cigarette dangling from my mouth, I threw a foot up on the edge of the bed and strapped the shotgun to my leg. "Maybe they do."

She shrugged, took a drag on her cigarette and exhaled through her nose. "Some say they keep the children out there because that's where they get older, and once they do, they come here. If that's true, that means we all come from there. We all grow up out there. So why can't we remember?"

I grabbed my coat. "Maybe we're not supposed to."

"Or maybe we're not allowed to, because it's all a lie and we were never there, because they never grow up and we never grow old. We all just…are."

She moved to the edge of the bed, letting the sheet fall as she rose to her knees. "Do you ever remember being anything other than what you are now? Can you remember being ten—or even five—years younger than you are right now?"

I couldn't, but I said nothing.

"They say a Dreamcatcher knows things the rest of us don't, that your kind isn't like the rest of us. Is that true?"

She looked so different now, her hair mussed, her makeup all but gone. I liked her better this way. I just wished she'd stop talking. "We're no different than anyone else," I said. "This is just what we do."

"But *why?*" she asked, her eyes suddenly moist. "*Why* do you do what you do?"

I pulled on my coat. "I don't make the rules."

"Who does? Tell me," she said, tears streaming her face. "*Please*, Monk."

"I don't know."

"Would you tell me if you did?"

"Why are you crying?"

"Because it's all so sad, isn't it? Isn't it all so sad?"

"Stop crying and listen to me." I reached out and wiped her tears away with my thumb. "Did Julia warn the men in the bar that I was coming?" She seemed to deflate just then, and a look of even greater hopelessness and despair washed over her. Gathering the sheet in around her, she covered herself again and slumped back, the cigarette burning in her hand as if she'd forgotten it was there. Maybe she had. "She said someone would be coming for her," the Dahlia eventually answered, sighing. "They knew it was only a matter of time before a Dreamcatcher showed up. We all did. But she never said it'd be her husband, never said it'd be you."

But she knew, I thought. *She knew.*

Julia's face came to me, her voice in my ear. *I'll always love you…always…but will you always love me?*

"If I were your wife," the Dahlia said, bottom lip quivering as she fought back more tears, "I wouldn't run away. I wouldn't betray you. Not ever."

"Sure you would. And who could blame you?"

I leaned closer, kissed her on the forehead, and said goodbye.

* * *

The rain had stopped earlier, but the night was alive with its memory. There were puddles everywhere and everything was soaked from the downpour.

I didn't see her until I'd left the building and rounded the side of the bar. Falcon. Or Eddie, to those of us who knew her. Falcon, because of her tattoos. Eddie, because her real name was Edna, but no one ever dared call her that. Had she come to kill me, I'd have already been dead. She was, without question, the best Dreamcatcher in the business. Some considered her the best there'd ever been, and I was among those who did.

Leaned against my car, arms folded over her chest, Falcon Eddie offered me a wry smile. Tall, thin and athletically built, she was clad in her usual thigh-high boots, black gloves, and one-piece outfit of black leather, the front zipped down to her midriff. An enormous tattoo of a falcon was perched between her small breasts, and her peroxide blonde hair, piled high on her head, was held in place with two ornate red sticks that looked like something you'd eat Chinese food with. For the uninitiated, at first glance it appeared as if her heavy, dark eye makeup was running, but closer inspection revealed the black streaks under her ice-blue eyes were actually matching tattoos of talons. Her look, while dynamic, was only for effect, to initially startle and frighten. The real horror was what she brought to the table, the real killer beneath the over-the-top outfits and tattoos.

"How goes it, Monk?" she asked evenly.

"What the hell are you doing here?"

"That was gonna be *my* next question."

"I'm off the clock."

"Well be a good little bunny and hop back on it for me then." Eddie's weapon of choice, a samurai sword, was strapped to her back, but she also had .45s holstered on both hips, and a series of throwing knives fitted into slits along her left arm, from her shoulder to just above her elbow. She'd always had a flair for the dramatic, but ironically enough, she was as lethal without her weapons as she was with them. I'd seen her kill with her bare hands more than once. "They want to see you at HQ. Cap's having himself a fucking aneurism."

"You some sort of message delivery girl now?"

Her topaz eyes turned even colder. "Tell you what, you see a *girl* anywhere around here, you slap her cute little bottom and send her home to her momma, motherfucker."

"Figure of speech," I said, taking a final drag on my cigarette before flicking it into the darkness. "Relax."

"You know me, Monk, relaxing ain't really my thing." Except for around her eyes, she wore no makeup, and other than her tattoos and a battle scar along her chin, her complexion was almost unnaturally smooth. "Like I said, they want you back at HQ."

"Why?"

"Don't waste my time. It does a number on what little patience I have to begin with, and makes me very angry."

"I'm not on the job. My time's my own."

"You gonna give me a hard time on this?" She sighed and shook her head. "Seriously, that's how you want to play it?"

I stood my ground.

"Saw your wheels from the road, followed the bodies right to you." Falcon Eddie cocked her head toward the bar. "Hell of a mess in there."

"These things happen."

"Gotta love the badge. Gives us permission to do anything we want. Almost."

"I told you, I'm not on the job."

"What are you doing out here then?"

I held her stare and went quiet again.

"You've never even been out this way, have you?" she pressed.

"None of my runners have ever made it this far."

Her eyes sparkled with amusement and a touch of respect. "Did you really think HQ wouldn't find out what was going on?"

"Eddie, look—"

"Julia's a runner," she said. "It's already been decided."

I rubbed the back of my neck, but it did little to relieve my rising tension. I'd hoped for more time. "She's not a runner. She's just—"

"She's a runner. And unless you come back to HQ with me, so are you."

"I need to find her and bring her home, all right? She's not running. She's confused, she's—"

"I understand she's your wife, okay?" Falcon Eddie pushed away from my car but was careful not to come too close. "I get it. You're in a shitty position. Cap ordered me to bring you back so we can all chalk this up to a simple misunderstanding. After all, it's not just some runner, it's your wife. You lost your head, got a little nuts is all. Come back with me now and all is forgiven."

"I'm asking you to cut me a break, Eddie. One professional to another, I'm asking. Tell them you couldn't find me. Tell them I was already into the outlands."

"You think that'd stop me?" she chuckled. "You think they'd *believe* that would stop me? Would it stop you? *Is* it stopping you?"

"I'm asking for a favor, all right? I'll pay it back however you see fit."

"Come on, you know how this works."

"I need some time. Give me one more night."

"Can't do it," she said. No hesitation; no thought. "If they run, we hunt them down. We bring them back. Dead or alive, but we bring them back. If they tell me to go get another Dreamcatcher that's lost his or her way and bring him or her home, that's what I do. Same as you would. Same as any of us would."

All I could think about were the countless faces that had looked at me the same way I was looking at her, the pleading voices asking for a chance, a break, a moment in time, the smallest scrap of mercy I might be able to throw their way. And as they'd seen in me, I saw no hope in her. It was just a job. We did what we did because that's what we'd been led to believe was what we were supposed to do. It was who we were. Our kind was necessary because we kept order, and our actions allowed the world to continue to exist as it was supposed to, or as we'd been taught it was supposed to. There were rules, and those rules had to be followed. If the rules were bent or broken, we were told, there would be nothing but chaos. But what was there now? If the world was already in flames, what was a little more gasoline on the fire? Could one be *more* damned, *more* doomed, *more* broken, *more* forgotten, *more* marginalized to the outskirts of existence? The reality was, we'd all been dropped into a meat grinder and told, regardless of the consequences, that if we questioned it in any way, we were attempting to destroy the natural order of things. We weren't simply criminals, we were heretics. And in the light or the dark, it didn't much matter, because heretics were for burning. Made no difference who lit the match or gave the order, that's the way things were, the way they'd always been and always would be. You did what you were told.

"Julia's not running," I said. "And neither am I."

"Do you think I'm gonna stand out here all night and discuss this with you?" She walked along the side of the car, parallel to me. "HQ already has a major root growing up their collective asses over the whole Frisco Sean and Matt the Cat bullshit. Can't be letting runners slip free. Doesn't matter who they are, you know that. You got any idea how much shit Dingo took for losing them?"

"I can imagine."

"Then you understand my position here."

"I'm asking you to understand mine," I said, but I was already trying to figure out how I was going to get away from her. Reasoning was obviously out, and that left force, which was a bad idea no matter how I came at it.

"Dingo's deep in the shit. They're gonna assign Julia to him, and if he drops the ball on this one, they already told him not to bother coming back. They'll just send someone else for him and her, and it'll be a BBD job."

Bring Back Dead, the kind of job where the runner was to be executed upon being located. No exceptions, no excuses. If they were BBD, they were to be killed without question or hesitation. No chance to come in alive.

"Is Dingo already on the clock?" I asked.

"Soon," Eddie said with a coy look. "I may have convinced Cap to wait to send him out until I brought you back and we found out exactly what was going on."

Eddie didn't know it, but that one show of respect on her part had bought me exactly what I needed. Time. None of it mattered if I went back with her, though, so I had to find a way to separate myself from her, and quickly, because if I could, her actions had bought me at least another night or two before they sent Dingo after us both. "You didn't have to do that," I said. "Thanks."

"You're right, I didn't. To be honest, I never really liked you—don't take it personally, I don't fucking like anybody—but I always respected you. You're good. Not as good as me, of course, but real good. I figured you at least deserved that much."

I moved closer. "I'd feel a hell of a lot better if they'd let me go after her."

"You know they'd never let you take this one."

Working the only angle I had, I said, "No, but they'd let you."

Falcon Eddie furrowed her brow. "I told you they already assigned it to Dingo."

"Dingo's an incompetent ass. If he fucks it up like he fucked up his last job—"

"In all fairness, he may not be our level, but it is the only one he's ever blown."

"If he loses Julia too, they both die. If you got the job, I know you'd find her, and I know you could bring her back alive."

"You want me to ask for the job, is that it?"

"They'll give it to you if you do."

"Done," she said, face expressionless. "If it'll get your ass in gear and back to HQ, I give you my word. Now let's move. They're not gonna wait forever, and they'll only keep Dingo on a short leash so long." She jerked her thumb at the huge silver chopper she always rode, which was parked on the other side of my car. "Take that bucket of shit you call a car. I'll follow you."

Though I was still trying to think a few moves ahead, I started toward the car slowly, so I could easily close the gap between us as I passed by her.

"One more little technicality," she said. "For your safety, and of course, mine."

I already knew what was coming.

"Gonna need you to turn your weapons over to me. Just until

we get back. They'll be returned to you once we get to HQ."

"That's not necessary."

"It is if I say it is. And I do."

"Fine," I said through a heavy sigh. I reached down, unstrapped the shotgun from my leg and held it out for her.

Falcon Eddie took it and slung it over her shoulder. "Keep going."

I gave her my best questioning look.

"You expect me to believe that's all you're packing?"

"Not everybody's the walking arsenal you are."

"Come on, let's go. Hand it over."

With another dramatic sigh I reached into my coat pocket and pulled out my revolver. Fumbling it, I dropped it to the ground between us, doing my best to make it appear as if I'd done so accidentally. Eddie didn't look like she'd bought it, but I kept playing my part anyway, and crouched down to get it.

The moment I touched the gun she stepped on my hand, pinning it to the ground with the heel of her boot. "I'll get it," she said. "Get in your car."

She stepped back, freeing my hand, and in one quick and fluid motion, I scooped up a handful of dirt, rose to my feet and threw it in her face.

As she staggered back a bit to avoid it, I swung at her hard as I could.

With ease, Eddie blocked my punches, knocking them away with speed and precision, even as she blinked and shook her head, still partially blinded from the dirt. I kept coming regardless, throwing combinations. None landed but they backed her up.

I was so focused on breaking through her hand blocks that I never saw the leg kick coming. It caught me on the side of my knee, nearly buckled it and sent daggers of pain up into my thigh and waist. Knocked off balance, I stumbled to the side, caught myself before I fell, then planted my foot, spun, and launched an elbow back at her. It connected with the bridge of her nose with a loud crack, and I heard her grunt.

In the mayhem, the shotgun had fallen from her shoulder and landed nearby. But the pistol was closer, so I turned and scrambled for it.

I got less than a step before she grabbed me by the back of my coat and yanked me toward her, slamming her other forearm into my neck.

The force of the blow snapped my head back, but before I could react, she spun me around to face her, brought a knee up into my stomach and followed up with a quick combination of punches to my jaw.

My legs checked out and down I went, collapsing into a puddle on my back. Head spinning and jaw aching, I rolled away as she stomped a boot heel where my throat had been a second before. On my side, I swung my leg hard, catching the back of her knee and buckling it. But as she dropped to her knees, she twisted at the waist and threw an elbow that smashed into my mouth and returned me to my back. I tasted blood and coughed, spraying crimson up into the darkness.

Eddie leaned closer and threw a hook into my side, below the rib cage. The blow knocked most of the wind out of me, but I crawled away as best I could.

"Stupid son of a bitch," she muttered, rising to her feet. "Are you out of your *fucking* mind?" She wiped her eyes, then checked her nose, which was bleeding from both nostrils. "Give me one reason why I shouldn't kill you right now!"

With the world still tilting and blurred, I forced myself to my hands and knees. When I tried to respond, I gagged on a mouthful of blood and spat it out into the mud along with one of my bottom teeth. A long drool of blood and spittle dangled from my quickly swelling bottom lip. I tried to speak again, and this time managed, "I have to get to her, Eddie, I—"

"Get in the fucking car!"

"I have to find her, I—"

Next thing I knew she'd grabbed hold of me and pulled me to my feet. After slapping me across the face, she came back around with a backhand and slapped me again. Then, shaking me like a rag doll, she pivoted and hip-tossed me.

I left my feet, crashed onto the hood of my car and lay there a moment. The black sky moved and swirled above me; a new series of pains stabbed at my temples and along my spine.

"Get in the fucking car, Monk," Eddie growled, chest heaving. "I'm not gonna tell you again, I'm just gonna end you. Right here, right now."

Despite the pain and the tricks my equilibrium was playing on me, I rolled off the hood and toppled to the ground with a grunt. Struggling, I reached up, grabbed the side mirror for leverage, and pulled myself to my feet. Steadying my stance as best I could, I spat out another streamer of blood.

"Don't do it," she warned.

I charged her again.

Eddie moved laterally, sliding to the side with the grace of a matador, then brought her leg up and kicked me dead in the center of the chest with her shin. Because I was charging, I ran right into it, and it sent me tumbling backward, somersaulting away and into the side of the car.

I rolled over, and with great effort, got back to my feet. I wasn't entirely sure where the hell I was, but once I'd located her, I raised my fists and staggered toward her a third time.

"Don't make me do this, Monk," she said, squaring her stance.

"You're gonna have to kill me," I slurred, slobbering more blood from my mouth.

Falcon Eddie reached behind her, slowly slid her sword free, and held it out in front of her, the tip of the long blade leveled at me. "So be it."

I was in a tremendous amount of pain—I was having trouble drawing a full breath, and I was hobbled from the kick to my knee—but my head was starting to clear, along with my vision Still, it was difficult to gauge precise distances in the mounting darkness. I circled her slowly, trying to settle on a plan of attack. She stood her ground, motionless, like she'd frozen in position. I was prepared to die if I had to, and figured I was probably only moments away from it anyway. The odds of me taking her out were nearly nonexistent—and we both knew it—but I had no other options. If I went back to HQ with her, Julia was gone and gone for good. Dead or alive, she was gone. And so was I. Better to go out swinging than to shuffle obediently back to my superiors and leave Julia's fate in someone else's hands.

My shotgun was quite a distance behind her now, but the pistol was still lying in the dirt a few feet away. I wasn't sure if I could get to it in time but I had to try.

"You won't make it," she said.

I bolted for the pistol.

In an instant, she was between me and the weapon, the sword still level and aimed at me. And then, for reasons I'll never understand, something changed in her eyes, and she stood down, relaxing her stance and lowering the sword to her side.

I rubbed my eyes and focused on her again, unable to believe what I'd just seen. But there she was, staring at me through the night with what I realized was pity.

After a lengthy silence she said, "You love her that much?"

"She's all I got, Eddie. She's everything."

"What's it like?"

I wasn't sure what she meant.

"Love," she said. "What's it like?"

I wondered if she saw pity in my eyes as well. "You've never felt it for anyone?"

She wiped a fresh trickle of blood from her nose, then shook her head in the negative. "Tell me. What's it like?"

I thought about it a moment. "Like dreaming. Like God dreaming."

A hint of a smile slipped across her face. There, then gone.

One of us was about to die, so we stood there a while with each other, amidst the quiet of a darkness neither of us truly understood or likely ever would, in a parking lot of dirt along the side of a deserted highway to nowhere, and everywhere.

"Listen to you, all poetic and shit," she finally said. "Romantic as that is, I still can't let you go. You know that, Monk, even better than I do."

I told her I did, and that there were no hard feelings.

Then I rushed her one final time.

This time I got close enough to get my hands on her, and I used my weight to gain enough leverage to force her back a few steps. Clutching each other, we wrestled for position, stumbling about together as I slid my hands up and onto her throat. But she managed to hook my leg with her foot and execute a judo toss that flipped me into the air. I crashed to the ground, landing flat on my back with tremendous force and a certainty that everything inside me had shattered.

I tried to get up but couldn't draw breath, so I began to squirm and writhe about until I'd forced myself onto my side, and then up and onto my knees. As a rush of breath returned to my lungs, I began to rise to my feet once again, but Eddie stepped in, hit me with a three-punch combination, then finished the job with a vicious spinning heel kick that evidently caught me on the side of the head.

The next thing I remembered was crawling out of unconsciousness and feeling sick to my stomach. A sense of panic and a rush of emotion surged through me as I realized I'd been knocked out and was just then coming to, unaware of exactly what had happened. Lying in the mud, I struggled back to my hands and knees, but was so dizzy I couldn't come anywhere near standing. I was done. It was over.

Falcon Eddie stood above me, the sword in her hands again.

Through swollen and bloodied eyes, I looked up at her and gave a slight nod, then bowed my head so she could take it off with a single swing of the blade. *Do it*, I thought. *For Christ's sake, just do it.*

"Didn't have to be like this," she said. "But you got my respect, Monk."

She widened her stance.

I closed my eyes.

And then, from what sounded like somewhere far away, there came an oddly familiar clicking sound, followed by a deafening boom.

I opened my eyes, still barely conscious, and saw Eddie standing there, her face ravaged by confusion. An enormous wound had blown out a section of her abdomen, and a length of intestines dangled from the gruesome cavity like bloody rope.

Behind her in the dark, the Dahlia stood holding my shotgun. It was still smoking.

Eddie dropped her sword and fell to her knees. Looking down at her stomach, she groggily tried to push her innards back in. The intestines slipped free of her weak grip, squishing and squirming about like blood-spattered eels. She vomited black blood and bile, swaying there on her knees with a look of utter disbelief. Then she fell back into the mud and lay still.

I fell forward onto my hands and crawled over to her.

She was still alive. "Not like this," she gasped, slurring the words as her chest began to wheeze and buck. "Not like this, Monk, not...please...not like this..."

I took her bloody hand in mine and held it tight. With my free hand, I slid one of her .45s from its holster and placed the barrel beneath her chin. Had I waited, she'd have been dead in minutes anyway, but she deserved better than to be taken out by an amateur she should've heard coming. This way, she'd die by my hand. To someone like Falcon Eddie, to someone like me, that made a world of difference.

She tried to speak again but it came out as an indecipherable gurgling sound.

We were still holding hands and looking directly into each other's eyes when I pulled the trigger and blew her brains out through the top of her head.

CHAPTER NINE

*I know nothing. In the silence of sorrow, I am an embryo float-
ing in murky fluid, unaware of how or why or when I have become,
what came before or what awaits me. With the voices of angels in my
mind, my eyes begin to see…I am sitting in a chair in an otherwise
empty room, my legs covered with a blanket. I am impossibly old,
and everything is so…white… the walls, the floors, the ceiling, all
of it an intensely dazzling white. I don't seem to notice, as I'm having trouble breathing, and I'm gasping, slowly taking in small gulps
of air. But it's not enough. I struggle to breathe, and I'm frightened,
which only makes it worse. I cannot breathe as I should, as I need to,
and although this is horrifying enough, there is something…else…
something in the room with me I cannot quite see. It lingers at the
edge of my peripheral vision, and for some reason, I cannot turn my
head to get a better look. Perhaps I don't want to, because whatever
it is, it's looking right at me, and I wish it would stop. I can feel its
eyes on me but I want it to go away and leave me alone. I can feel*

the evil within it, profane and unclean as it considers me the way one contemplates an insect prior to stepping on it. But it makes no sound, as except for my wheezing and gasping, it is especially quiet here in this strange little room of blinding light and forgotten toys.

Suddenly, before me, there is something more beyond the light. Not behind me or to the side, but straight ahead, through a thin plate of flawless glass, it moves with a majesty and beauty I cannot even begin to comprehend. Such colors and vibrancy I have never seen or even imagined. Is it a dream? Or am I what it dreams of? This mother of all things, so close I can smell it…but still beyond my reach, my touch…it makes me want to weep, because I know now that there is a God, and I am in its presence. I have been all along. And I am no longer afraid.

I am ashamed.

* * *

I tossed the .45 into the night and tried to get to my feet. I managed it on the third attempt, but I was still shaky. Bloody, battered and nauseated, I stumbled over to the Dahlia, who was still frozen and holding the shotgun as if she'd drifted into a trance. I gently took the weapon from her. Doing so broke the spell, and she began to tremble and quake, her eyes streaming tears.

"She would've killed you," she said softly.

I put my hands on her shoulders, hoping to steady us both. "Listen to me," I said. "When—"

"There was nothing else I could do, she was going to—"

"*Listen* to me," I snapped, tightening my grip on her shoulders. "When they come…and they *will* come…you tell them I did this, that I shot her in the back, then finished her off. They'll believe you. Do you understand?"

She stared at me through her tears.

"*Do you understand?*"

"Yes."

No one ever stepped up to save a Dreamcatcher; they cheered

90

when my kind was killed and called it justice. But the Dahlia had saved my life and put her own in severe jeopardy, and I wished there was something more I could do for her. But there wasn't. We were slaves, nothing more. I leaned closer, until our foreheads touched, and felt her arms wrap around my back. "Thank you," I whispered.

"Are you all right?"

"Yeah," I lied.

"I wish you'd take me with you."

"No." I kissed her pale cheek, smearing it with blood. "You don't."

I gathered my weapons and managed to get back to my car without collapsing.

I left the Dahlia on the side of the road.

The last time I saw her, it was in my rearview. She was standing in the dirt like the lost waif she was, an orphan in the dark watching me go, until the night had swallowed her whole.

Head spinning and body aching, I sped into the outlands.

And one step closer to Julia.

* * *

For miles and what was surely hours, I drove through nothing but wasteland and darkness. Illuminated by the headlights, serpentine shapes of dirt and sand slinked across the highway from the dead land on either side of the road, skittering across the asphalt like snakes. But nothing else moved. Nothing else lived.

Eventually, the outskirts of a city appeared in the distance, emerging from the darkness. At first I thought I must be seeing things—*a city out here?*—but it was right there before my eyes, and I was headed straight for it. Nowhere near the size of my hometown, with the exception of two tall smokestacks, it lacked the giant spires rising high into the sky, the predominantly black steel architecture, the trains and sky trams, and consisted instead of smaller buildings spread out over a vast stretch of wasteland.

At the edge of the city, I pulled into the dirt lot of a gas station and slid in alongside the pumps. Head pounding, I forced myself out of the car and tried to get my bearings. I hurt everywhere, and my gums throbbed where my tooth had snapped off earlier. I spat into the night, threw on the closest gas pump, pushed the nozzle into the tank and let it flow. No one came out, and the building, while lit from the inside, appeared empty.

Once my tank was full, I ventured inside in the hopes of finding someone, but the station was deserted. I found a key attached to a chunk of wood marked RESTROOM hanging from a hook behind the counter, so I grabbed it and made my way around the side of the building to the bathrooms.

A filthy tile floor welcomed me, along with an equally filthy double sink, mirror and toilet stalls. The smell of the place matched its look. Overhead, a set of fluorescent lights buzzed and flickered, bathing the room in a strange hue. I got a look at myself in the mirror and immediately slumped against the sinks. The beating I'd taken earlier had not only left me exhausted and racked with pain, but with the cuts and bruises to prove it. I turned on the faucet. Water with a brown tint burst and spit forth as I reached into my mouth and checked my teeth. Except for the one I'd lost, they were all intact, although one molar felt a bit loose. I figured it wasn't going anywhere anytime soon, so I left it alone. But my hand came back bloody, so I scooped a handful of water from the faucet and rinsed out my mouth. Spitting the whole mess back into the sink, I watched the blood and dingy water gurgle down the grimy, rusted drain, then worked my head slowly back and forth in an attempt to ease the pain at the base of my neck. It did little to relieve it. I next inspected the wounds on my face, lightly touching the cuts above my right eye—which had stopped bleeding some time ago but were now caked with dried blood—and the purple and black bruises above my left. After splashing another handful or two of water on my face and washing off my eyes, I moved to my nose. My nostrils were ringed and flecked with more dried blood. I took hold of the bridge of my nose and moved it to the left, then right. It hurt but didn't begin to bleed again or make any crackling sounds. I wiped away the dried blood, then inspected my jaw, which hurt and felt as if it had been knocked out of line, but seemed to move and function as it should. Another dark bruise, along with a scrape, stretched from my temple to the side of my face, courtesy of Eddie's kick. I touched it carefully and winced in pain. It looked bad, but nothing was broken. My hands were bloody from numerous scrapes and cuts along my knuckles, so I washed them off as best I could and worked all ten fingers and both wrists until most of the stiffness and pain had ceased. Thankfully, again, nothing was broken.

Limping from the kick to my knee, I left the bathroom and returned to the station. I was still alone, so I tossed the key on the counter and headed back to my car.

Back behind the wheel, I lit a cigarette and considered things a moment. Did I want to go through this strange city I had never been to, or was it better to go around it and continue deeper into the outlands? Which one did Julia choose? I wondered. By the time I finished my smoke, I'd decided to drive straight through the heart of the city.

The moment I reached the main boulevard, I realized the city was empty too. No one on the streets, nothing moving, block after block of empty sidewalks, dark and silent buildings on either side of me, cars and various vehicles parked and unmanned, debris and trash blowing about in the night breeze. Were it not for the occasional murky streetlight, the entire city would've been cloaked in darkness.

I slowed the car and crept along the avenue, my eyes darting back and forth in an attempt to keep as much of the area in sight as possible. But the deeper into the city I drove, the more I began to understand that something was wrong. If this was a dead and abandoned city, why was everything in such relatively good shape? Some neighborhoods were worse than others, of course; but overall, the city looked as if it was occupied. Much like my own, it also *looked* as if it was slowly wasting away, yet somehow still maintained on a menial level.

You've never even been out this way, have you?

It didn't seem possible I'd been…alive…as long as I had and had never ventured this far from the city. But I hadn't. And until that moment in time I'd never questioned it.

As I moved slowly through the city, I couldn't shake Falcon Eddie's question. And all that did was open the floodgates for those the Dahlia had asked.

Do you remember being a child?

I turned at the corner onto another wide drag, but found more of the same.

Why do you think that is?

But I did have memories. Didn't I? They were vague and not always in context, but I did have them, I…

Why can't we remember?

It's just the way it was. When people worked, they rarely remembered how they got there or what led up to it, they were simply there and doing their thing. The Dahlia had said that. I'd once gone with Julia to see her mother who was not her mother, and I couldn't quite remember either. Certainly something had led up to our being there, and something had happened when it was over. But I had no memories of either.

Do you ever remember being anything other than what you are now?

I ran a hand through my hair. It came back damp with sweat. These were the thoughts and questions that started problems. That's what I'd been taught. You didn't question, you did your job—and we all had jobs to do—because questioning how things were, or the laws, or how they'd come to be and who was behind them accomplished nothing but discontent, and moved people closer to being runners. And runners were nothing to aspire to. To question was to conspire against creation and the way of the world, the way things were meant to be, the way things *had* to be.

Or so I'd thought. Maybe I was wrong. Maybe I'd been wrong all along.

Maybe the runners had it right. Maybe we didn't have to

populate the dreams of the others. But if not us, didn't someone? Or had the Dahlia been right? Had we been lied to all along? Fooled into believing things that were not necessarily so?

I was gripping the steering wheel so tight my palm had begun to hurt. I eased up and rolled along another block of quiet buildings and empty vehicles.

The only thing I knew for sure was that none of it mattered without Julia.

It suddenly occurred to me that the dull streetlights I'd seen earlier were gone. This street was pitch-black, so I grabbed a flashlight from my glove compartment and aimed it out the driver's side window. Without realizing it, I'd ventured into a much worse neighborhood that consisted largely of blown-out buildings and run-down storefronts that looked as if they hadn't been occupied in ages. The beam from the flashlight swept slowly through the darkness, eerily revealing small portions of the street at a time and eventually illuminating a lot where a large brick building had once stood. It had long since been reduced to rubble and piles of bricks scattered throughout the lot, and on either side of it stood two abandoned, barely standing tenements.

In the narrow alley between the next two buildings, something suddenly glowed at me through the night. A pair of eyes reflecting the flashlight beam. I stepped on the brake, slowing the car to a stop, jammed it into Park and stepped out.

With a quick look around, I walked toward the sidewalk, the flashlight out in front of me and my other hand clutching the pistol in my coat pocket. The eyes remained where they were, unmoving but blinking occasionally. I walked across rubble and debris and onto the sidewalk. In the alley, the pair of eyes became an old man huddled in the darkness, looking up at me with a mixture of fear and curiosity.

"Come out of there," I ordered.

"I'd surely like to oblige, mister," a gravelly voice answered, the words slurred. "But I don't believe I can stand up just now."

I looked to my left, then right, sweeping the flashlight as I did. The street was empty and quiet. Nothing moved but the beam of light.

"Don't worry," the old man said, "they're all sleeping."

Moving closer to the alley, I leveled the light at him. "Who?"

"Why, the rest of the people, of course." He shielded his eyes with a liver-spotted hand gnarled with arthritis. "Sure would appreciate it if you wouldn't aim that right at my face, mister."

I lowered it a bit. When I took a step closer, I realized why he couldn't stand. The stench of cheap booze drifted up out of the alley and hit me, mixed with the smell of body odor and urine. "They're asleep?"

He nodded, brought a brown bottle of liquor to his mouth and took a long pull. With a loose, rumbling cough, he wiped at his mouth with his bad hand, then scratched maniacally at his cheek, which was covered in stubble and several scabs. "I'm the only one awake now."

"What is this place?"

"Photas," he said, coughing again.

I'd heard rumors, but most of us believed the city of Photas was a myth. And yet, if this drunken old homeless man was telling the truth, it not only existed, it had been closer than I'd ever imagined possible all along. "City of the Night Sleepers," I said.

"Yes, sir," the old man answered. "They're like the others. They sleep in the night and live in the daylight. Somebody's got to tend to the others that sleep in the day, or even the Night Sleepers that sometimes sleep in the day, see?"

"Then what about you?"

"I used to be one of those freaks," he said, "but not anymore. Not in a long time."

"But if you're one of them, how did you change?"

He held up the bottle and smiled wide. Not a tooth in his head. "Found salvation in my magic elixir here, friend. Helped me see the darkness and made me realize I didn't have to be like that. I'm just a bum. Far as they're concerned, *I'm* the freak.

They don't understand how beautiful the night is, and they never will. But you and me, friend, we know different, don't we."

"You mean to tell me you just *stopped* sleeping at night?"

"Sure did."

"And nothing happened?"

"Like what?" He shrugged. "I hardly ever work anymore anyway. Nobody pays me any mind. They think I'm some sort of wizard or something. Some even claim I'm a demon."

I tightened my grip on the pistol in my pocket. "Are you?"

"I'm just an old man, son."

Madness, I thought, *how could it be that simple?*

Like he'd been suddenly reminded of something else, he ran his mangled hand across his face, touching the array of scabs littering his cheeks, chin and neck with his fingers. "Been *changing*, though, must say."

"Changing how?"

"My eyes," he said. "And my skin—it's changed since I became a day sleeper. When we work, we all look the same, but the rest of the time we look different. Now I'm becoming more and more like that all the time. More like you, less like them... me."

"Why do you stay here?" I asked.

"I got nowhere else to go and no way to get there if I did. Truth is, mister, most nights I don't walk so good anymore."

Despite the stench, I stepped closer and crouched down next to him. Slowly, I panned the flashlight across him. His white hair was thin and mussed, and his clothes were tattered, filthy. He wore no shoes, and his feet were scarred and diseased, the toes unkempt, filthy and mangled with arthritis.

Until that moment, I'd only heard about his kind in ghost stories, Night Sleepers and their city of light. But it was all right here in the dark with the rest of us.

"You know what I am?" I asked.

"With those wounds you look like a man of violence." He watched me with his bloodshot eyes, took a swig of booze, then belched. "Dreamcatcher, I'd imagine."

There had always been rumors that a secret department existed within HQ that catered exclusively to the Night Sleepers and their runners, but I'd never seen proof of any of it. It was whispers in hallways, innuendo, stories someone heard from someone else or paperwork an associate of an associate had allegedly seen.

"Then you know I'm looking for someone."

"Yes, sir, I'd imagine that too." He held the bottle out for me. "Drink?"

Much as I needed a drink, I waved it away. "Looking for a woman."

"I wish I could help you, mister. But I promise you I can't."

"Her name's Julia. Did she come through here?"

"If she did, I never saw her. You're the only stranger I've seen in a long time."

I brought the light back up to his face. "You telling me the truth, old-timer?"

This time he made no effort to shield his eyes. "Son, why would I lie to you?"

I stood up and took another quick look around to make sure we were still alone. In the nearby lot I could hear rats squeaking and scurrying about in the ruins. I looked back at my car and the sky beyond the buildings on the far side of the street. Things were changing. Slowly, gradually, like always, one world dying as another was reborn. "It'll be daytime soon," I said.

"You'll want to be gone by the time the light comes," he told me.

"I'll be asleep by then."

"Be asleep far away, son. You don't want to be here when they wake up."

The night was dying, the streetlights on the next block fading. *Chaos*, I thought. *It's all chaos here and probably worse the farther out I go.* There was supposed to be order—reason and organization; things were supposed to make sense—but the deeper I looked, the less order I saw. Instead, it seemed more like a haphazard and lawless dream world where nothing made sense, no one knew what to do or how to control it, much less escape it, and that the confines of the city and nearby areas I'd existed in for so long were only constructs of fantasy and distraction. What the hell were we doing here? Why were we here in the first place, in this godforsaken wasteland of nightmares, magic and emptiness? I'd always been so certain there had to be a reason for all of it, for all of *us*. Now I could no longer be quite so sure.

I pictured Lenore laughing in her filthy little sex palace…

We are *parlor tricks.*

Dead flies falling all around her…

Rumors whispered in the rain…in darkness…

As she opened her legs and lived out her depraved fairy tales…

Actors performing in empty theaters…

"If the woman I'm looking for is here, where would she—"

"If she passed through at night, there's a chance she's alive," he interrupted, battling another gurgling coughing fit. "If she was still here in the light, she's dead."

A strange rumbling sound cut the silence as the city trembled beneath my feet. In the distance, through the darkness, enormous bursts of white smoke suddenly appeared from a pair of stacks several blocks away. By far the tallest pieces of architecture in the city, they towered above the streets like giant sentries come to life, growling and spitting their dreams across a city that was sure to follow.

"The machines," the old man said ominously, "they're awake."

I took my cigarettes from my pocket, lit one and handed it to him. "Others will be coming," I told him. "More of my kind, and they'll be looking for me, understand?"

He nodded. "I didn't see nothing, friend." Greedily drawing on the cigarette, he grimaced, then hacked out a cloud of smoke. "But go. Now, while you still can. You have no idea what they do to strangers here."

In the windows of what I had assumed was an abandoned building across the street, faces emerged. Faces with leathery, reptilian-like skin, hair like straw and the blackest eyes I had ever seen—no irises, only cold black orbs staring at me—they watched and waited.

"For God's sake, son," the old man said. "*Go.*"

With the night slowly burning away, and the legendary city of Photas coming alive all around me, I turned and hobbled for the car.

CHAPTER TEN

Even in fear, in danger, and in violence, the world was barren, void of what it was to be truly alive. A living world, as it were, didn't exist here. It never had. In its place, there was only the primal, a reality in tatters. Tangled in the same webs that always imprisoned me, the same obsessions that had lorded over and driven me for as long as my memories existed, I barreled through the streets of Photas.

As daylight continued to gradually pierce the darkness, the inhabitants of the city awakened en masse, like pieces of a larger organism, a greater single consciousness. Suddenly those hideous scaled faces were everywhere, their black eyes staring at me from windows and doorways, alleys and rooftops. Human, and yet...

I took the next corner at high speed, pulling onto a long boulevard, tires screeching as the car skidded to the side before I was able to correct it. Once I had, I shot forward, pushing my old car hard as a wave of city dwellers emerged from buildings on either side and rushed into the street. Swerving back and forth, I managed to avoid the first several, who ran into my path without any regard for their safety, single-minded in their goal to prevent my escape, most waving about planks of wood or machetes, some even sporting rifles.

By the time I'd reached the end of the next street there were even more of them, their leathery faces and onyx eyes coming at me through the dying night and darting out from every direction as they swarmed from buildings and alleyways, emptying into the streets like a hive of agitated insects. Beyond the thudding of my heart, I heard an eerie and horrifying high-pitched shriek, and realized it was coming from them as they rushed the car. A war cry, perhaps, or some means of communication. I couldn't be sure which, and didn't care. I stomped the gas and rocketed straight for the growing crowd of Night Sleepers, certain they'd save themselves and move out of the way.

They didn't.

I plowed straight through them, their bodies bouncing up and over the hood. One, and then another, rolled and crashed into the windshield before falling away into what darkness still remained, while two others vanished beneath the hood, the car bouncing, tilting and shaking as I ran over their bodies, the mangled remains in my rearview sprawled in the street. I dragged another nearly a block before he finally fell free and rolled toward the gutter, swallowed by shadows as he bounced away in a cartwheel-like tumble.

The car sputtered and coughed as I took another corner and finally found the way out. I could see the highway and the slowly changing sky awaiting me, stretched out over endless miles of wasteland.

Speeding from the city, I hit the wipers, cleared the cracked windshield of blood and other debris, then checked my rearview again. No trace of the Night Sleepers.

The car sputtered again, so I slowed my speed and gave the dashboard a reassuring pat. The old girl owed me nothing.

When I'd been on the highway for several minutes, and hadn't seen any sign of the Night Sleepers, I finally began to relax. They wanted to tear me limb from limb for crossing into their territory, but evidently not enough to venture this far beyond their beloved city of light.

I lit a cigarette and smoked it, trying to purge the visions of lizard skin and black eyes from my mind. Horrific, what the light did to them. I never thought I would, but I missed the city—mine, not theirs—the comfort of its familiar darkness, its streets and alleys I knew so well, its inhabitants, the neon and blood and cum.

Visions of the Night Sleepers were replaced by Joey the Creep vaulting backward off a roof in a spray of blood after I'd shot him in the face.

The evil you know.

The more daylight began to win, the better I could see. In fact, I could see for miles. The highway lay stretched out before me, the distant horizon offering nothing but empty wasteland, until something emerged from the scrub brush and otherwise flat landscape. A tree, perhaps sixty yards or so from the side of the road, it stood alone and out of place in the wilderness. Long dead, its branches were gnarled and bare and reached for the sky like the hand of a dead giant.

I slowed the car and pulled over, leaving the highway and driving carefully over the rough terrain. Once behind the tree, I parked, and with a weary sigh, climbed out of the car.

Exhausted, hungry and feeling sick, I gazed back down at the stretch of road from which I'd come. It remained empty, with no sign of my pursuers or anyone else.

By the time I'd finished my smoke, the night was almost gone.

My nerves had leveled off, so I removed my coat, climbed into the backseat of the car, locked the doors and covered myself, pulling the coat up over my face.

Then I closed my eyes and drifted away, hopeful I could escape the daylight and sleep straight through to night without incident.

* * *

"What about our dreams?"

I roll over and look into her eyes. In candlelight, she's more beautiful than ever, lying there next to me on her side, nude, with her hair draped across her face and down along her delicate shoulders, head resting on hands set palm-to-palm and flat against the mattress.

"What about them?" I ask.

Rather than answer, she stays quiet. The sound of a delicate rain hitting the building and tapping the windows fills the silence of our tiny apartment, as my eyes drift past her, over her shoulder to the desk and chair on the far wall. My weapons, still in various holsters, are draped across the chair, hanging there like the discarded tools of destruction they are.

"They don't exist," she says.

"I dream."

"No. You don't. And I don't either. None of us do."

I think about this a moment. It doesn't seem possible. Everyone dreams. Don't they? I try to remember one, but can't. Yet I feel as though I dream, as though I have.

"It's not possible here," she says. "Not for us."

And then it comes to me…the dream about her on the beach with the others. I don't tell her about it right away. Instead, I wait, and try to remember as much of it as I can. "I dream," I tell her again. "I dream about you."

Julia smiles. "Of course you do. But it's not real."

"I remember it. Doesn't that make it real?"

"You only think you remember it," she says.

"I dreamed about you on a beach, near an ocean. It had to be a dream. Those things don't exist in the real world."

"Maybe they do. Maybe everything we think we know is a lie. Just like our memories, maybe it's all bullshit."

I look deep into her eyes and try to see beyond the beauty that mesmerizes me. There is a soul behind them, I'm sure of it, and in that moment, I need to see that part of her, that depth. I need to know it exists, because if it exists in her, then maybe it exists in me too. "You shouldn't say things like that," I tell her softly. "Thinking like that and about these sorts of things only leads to trouble."

"Just accept," she says, sarcastically reciting the law. "Do not question."

"There has to be order, Julia. Without order there's only chaos."

She raises her head, looking at me as if I'm a stranger. Perhaps just then, I am. "You think this is order?"

I lie flat on my back and stare at the ceiling, studying cracks in the plaster. From a beautifully intricate web in the corner, a black spider emerges, crawling sluggishly closer. I wonder if it knows what it is, where it is. Or does it wonder the same of us?

In the nights just before she runs, Julia is more distant than usual. The closer I get to her, the farther away she seems, and this rainy night is no different. All I want to do is hold her and tell her how much I love her, to lose myself in her and everything she means to me. But she won't allow it.

"Do you remember your parents?" she asks.

I try not to be too obvious about it, but I look over at the old framed photographs on my desk. A black-and-white version of my mother and father stare back at me, posed formally, my mother seated with my father standing behind her, hands resting gently on her shoulders. My father was a stern man and a strict disciplinarian I was never close to. My mother, Gideon, though sometimes aloof, is loving and attentive. "Of course I do," I answer. "I remember lots of things."

"Like your childhood?"

"Yes."

"And your puppy?"

"You know I don't like to talk about that." I don't like to think about the dog I had as a child because it upsets me. Sometimes when I'm alone, the memories even make me cry. I loved my dog and I miss him terribly. Whenever I think of him, I remember how sad his eyes looked whenever I had to leave, and how excited he was when I returned. I remember when he grew old and died in my arms.

"Have you ever listened to the stories about the world of light?"

105

Julia asks. "I mean really listened."

"No such place exists. Not for us."

"What if it does?"

"It doesn't. It's just fairy tales."

"What about the others? What about their world?"

"We're not of that world, but this one."

"Maybe it's all one world," she says.

The spider begins to descend on its web, dropping from the ceiling and slowly coming closer.

I reach over to the nightstand and grab my lighter. When the spider is within reach, I spark the flame and hold it up beneath the creature. It senses the heat, immediately recoils and glides back up to the ceiling. After a moment, it slowly returns to its web in the corner, and the safety it has no choice but to believe it represents.

And I know exactly how it feels.

* * *

I came awake suddenly, but remained still. Instinct told me I was no longer alone. Slowly, I peeked out from behind my coat and allowed a moment for my eyes to adjust. I couldn't see anything beyond the windows, as night had returned, but I could hear the faint shuffling of feet outside the car, and a low murmur of whispers.

The doors were locked, so I had the option of quickly climbing back over into the front seat, then starting the car and getting the hell out of there, but I could tell from the nearby sounds that whoever or whatever had converged on my car had not come alone. There was no way to know for sure how many were out there, so I gripped the shotgun on my leg and slowly pulled it free.

In a single motion, I sat up, threw the coat aside and pushed open the car door. As I slid forward onto my feet and into the darkness, a flurry of movement exploded all around me, and in my peripheral vision, I saw the sparks and undulating flames from torches. I leveled the shotgun at the flames, then panned over to the shadows. Those within them scurried about, circling me.

"Who's there?" I called.

I nearly fired into the night, but then something small broke through the darkness, moving slowly into the light cast from the interior of the car. A little girl—no more than five or six— with a dirty face and hands, her strawberry blonde hair long and mussed, matted and in need of a thorough scrubbing; she was barefoot and clad in a worn and badly faded flowery dress. Behind the little waif I saw others, peering at me through the darkness with sad little eyes, and beyond them, others still, a bit older, holding torches.

I lowered the gun, but held it down against my side rather than returning it to the holster. "Who are you?" I asked the little girl, my voice groggy and still escaping sleep.

She cocked her head and looked at me as if she wasn't quite sure what to make of me. "I'm Amy," she said in a tiny sweet voice. "What's your name?"

"Monk," I said.

"That's a funny name. Like monkey? I've never seen a real monkey. I don't know if I would like monkeys. They're cute but kind of scary too, don't you think?"

More children emerged from the shadows. Their bright and flaming torches better illuminated the area and allowed me to see that there were even more children deeper in the darkness behind them. Most of the torchbearers were older, eleven or twelve, from the look. That was the cutoff. Except for when they were working, children twelve and under were segregated and kept together, while those thirteen and older were considered young adults and lived among the general population.

"How many of you are there?" I asked.

"I don't know," Amy said softly. "I can't count that high yet."

"Where am I?"

"Are you lost?"

"Not exactly, I..." I quickly wiped my eyes. "Do all of you live here?"

"Back there," Amy said, pointing behind her. "Down in the valley."

An older boy pushed through the others, his face filthy and his hair as badly matted as Amy's. All these children looked horribly unkempt and less than healthy, but this one in particular had an air about him that made me nervous. He moved and held himself with more confidence than seemed warranted given his slight build. Worse, he had a rifle in his hands. I looked beyond him to the others, and realized he wasn't the only one holding a gun. *Christ*, I thought, *the little fuckers are packed.*

"What are you doing out here?" he asked.

Every muscle in my body ached. I still couldn't put full weight on the leg Eddie had damaged without feeling extreme pain, and I was weak and run-down from the beating. But I'd learned long ago to mask my pain or injuries, and hoped I could pull it off this time. "Looking for someone," I answered in a gruff voice.

The boy sized me up, thoroughly unimpressed.

I carefully reached into my jacket pocket for the photograph of Julia, then held it out so he could see it. "This woman," I explained. "I'm looking for her."

His eyes shifted and something in his expression changed.

Before I could question him further, Amy happily blurted, "That's Julia!"

The boy flashed an angry look her way and Amy's smile faded.

"Yes," I said, returning the photo to my coat. "*Julia.* Is she with you?"

"No," the boy answered for her.

"I'm not looking to hurt her," I told him. "I just need to find her."

"She left," he said. "Last night."

"Was she alone?"

"She's a nice lady," Amy said.

"Yes," I said, "she is. Do you know where she went?"

"No more talking." The boy held a hand out. "Give me your gun."

"That's not gonna happen, son."

He pointed the rifle at me without hesitation, his hands so steady it was chilling. This wasn't the first time he'd aimed a gun at someone, and he'd likely fired it as well. There was a look in his eyes that wasn't quite right, animalistic and raw, primal at the edges. "I'm not your son," he said evenly.

"You're in charge then, is that it?" I asked him.

He nodded proudly.

"What's your name?"

"Chael."

"Okay, Chael. Look." I slid the shotgun into its holster. "It's put away and—"

"Give it to us right now," the little bastard cracked. "Or we'll take it from you."

The horde of children moved closer. They'd already surrounded the car and were at least seven or eight deep all the way around. None of them looked particularly friendly except for Amy. I didn't kill children and wanted to avoid a confrontation if at all possible, but given the shape I was in, after the beating Eddie had given me, I wasn't sure I could fend off so many of them even if I wanted to. Still, handing over all my weapons was out of the question. "Do you know what I am?" I asked.

"Yes."

"Then you know I'm not someone you want to be fucking around with."

The flames played across his face, giving him a more frightening look than he probably deserved. "Neither am I."

The crowd shifted, closing in around me.

Amy smiled a nearly toothless grin and reached out her hand. "Come with us."

I glanced down at her but didn't answer.

Chael's expression remained defiant. He took Amy's hand, and together, they backed up, deeper into the crowd, his eyes locked on mine. "Take him."

The children were on me before his orders had fully registered, and suddenly there were countless dirty faces rushing toward me, little hands pulling and pushing and punching. Some of the children dove for my legs, buckling my knees with their combined weight and dragging me down, clawing at me, a mass of tiny fists pounding away as I fell. Still in disbelief that this could actually be happening, I tried to squirm free, but one of them hit me with a blunt object on the back of my head, and I felt myself slipping into unconsciousness. My body rose, lifted up by all those small hands as they carried me off into the night.

And then darkness closed over me as the crowd surged once more, moving as one toward the valley in the distance, and whatever awaited us there.

CHAPTER ELEVEN

I faded in and out of consciousness, but was too weak and disoriented to fight back. Below, in the small valley, several fires burned. The crowd of children silently carried me down a slope and into the heart of the village they apparently called home. I came awake at one point to find us moving through the night and into the town proper, which consisted of numerous squat hut-like structures with rounded roofs and wooden doors. Through the darkness, the flames and my blurred vision, I saw countless large posts surrounding the village, the ends sharpened into points by crude but effective tools. Their purpose eluded me at first, as the only protection they could offer the village was from something coming directly out of the sky, but as we drifted down the wide dirt road that ran the length of the small town, it became evident why the posts had been honed to fine points.

On several, severed human heads were on display—adult

men and women both—thrust down onto the points and held in place, the gruesome expressions of most frozen in agony or shock, eyes long dead but still wide with horror. Others who had come before me, no doubt, unfortunate enough to cross into a place they didn't belong and had no means of escaping. The children paid no attention to the gory trophies, but my worst fears were realized in that moment, and I knew then that I had to get out of this place as soon as possible. This may have been a village of children, but these were clearly not innocents. Like damn near everywhere else, this was a place of death and despair.

As fear and horror throttled me, I struggled to free myself of this nightmare. But there was no escape, and I couldn't get my body to respond. I simply lay there in their little hands, limp as a rag doll.

My last thought before I fell again into unconsciousness was wondering if Julia had ever truly left this place alive.

"*Take him to the witch!*"

At first I couldn't be sure if I'd been knocked out again or simply been dropped to the ground. All I knew for sure was that I'd awakened on my back, and above me, the night sky blurred, drifting back and forth and rippling like liquid.

"Don't be afraid," I heard Amy say, though I couldn't see her.

I realized then I was on the ground. Instinctively, my hand reached for the shotgun. The holster was empty. I still had the revolver in my coat but didn't reach for it. If they hadn't searched me, it was still there and I didn't want them to know I had it. I tried to stand but my body wouldn't cooperate. I tried to speak but the words came out nonsensical and slurred.

Giggles, whispers and eerie little voices circled me in the darkness.

And then, despite my best efforts, the night took me again.

* * *

Take him to the witch…

The world returned slowly. My eyes adjusted, and along with

the other aches and pains already riddling my body, I now had a dull thumping pain in the back of my skull that ran all the way down the back of my neck and fanned out across my shoulder blades. The night sky was no longer above me, but instead a thatched ceiling. I tried to swallow, choked, then coughed. I wanted to raise my head, but when I tried, the pain became unbearable, so I stayed put.

Nearby I could hear the popping and burning from a fire, and smelled the smoke along with other peculiar smells I couldn't indentify. My head lolled to the side and I blinked rapidly until my vision began to sharpen and clear.

A makeshift fireplace…a fire burning within…a thin sheen of smoke filling the air…and someone kneeling before it, a woman dressed in a flowing black skirt fanned out along the dirt floor, a faded and dirty white blouse and a long veil on her head. She was murmuring in a quiet monotone, repeating strange words in a language I'd never heard, again and again, slowly rocking her body back and forth.

"Who are you?" I heard myself say. My voice sounded foreign, raspy and beaten down, the words slurred.

Slowly, the woman turned and looked back over her shoulder. A veil fell across her face as well, but it was white and sheer, revealing only glimpses of the face behind it.

"The children," I gasped. "They brought me here?"

The woman turned back to the fire. "Those aren't children," she said, her voice deep and sounding as if she'd just swallowed broken glass.

My head was clearing, albeit slowly, and my strength was returning. I tried again to raise my head, and although the pain was excruciating, I was able to do so. My eyes drifted along the mud walls and the dirt floor, over to where a makeshift wooden table and chairs sat, to the strange talismans covering the walls, what appeared to be human bones along with sticks and stones arranged into various hideous forms and shapes.

"Who are you?" I asked again, this time more urgently.

The woman mumbled another of her twisted prayers, then

threw something into the fire, which made it burn suddenly faster and hotter, the flames rising in height as sparks flew about the hut.

"I have many names," she gurgled.

I struggled onto my side, but standing was still out of the question. Nausea and dizziness left me weak and disoriented. "Hell is this place?" I growled.

"What do you think it is, Dreamcatcher?"

"Where are they?"

"Out there," she said, "in the dark."

With tremendous effort, I was able to get myself into an upright sitting position, and though a wave of dizziness swept through me, I managed to stay that way. "What are they doing?"

"Deciding whether you live or die."

"You're *with* them?"

"I'm trapped here."

I looked around the hut. "You're the witch I heard them whispering about."

"I am Chthonia."

"Hell's that mean?"

The woman slowly rose to her feet. Small of stature, she turned and faced me. Her hands were badly gnarled with arthritis, the fingers bent and crooked at horrible angles. "*Of the underworld*," she said.

Despite the pain, I couldn't help but chuckle. "Aren't we all?"

"They are legion."

I rubbed the back of my neck but it did little to ease the pain. "The spikes out there, the heads, they—"

"You *are* violence, Dreamcatcher, why should such things bother your kind?"

My vision clear, I could see her haggard face beneath the white veil, but there was something wrong with her eyes. Were they closed? "Yet your head is still on your shoulders," I said.

"They think I can protect them."

"Can you?"

"As with all things, time will tell."

"If you're really a witch, why not use your magic to escape?"

Chthonia reached for her veil with her mangled hands, slowly lifting it to reveal her face. The skin was pale and deeply lined, her features aged and unhealthy-looking. But it was her eyes that stopped me cold. She had none; only a gruesome swath of pink scar tissue where they should have been, where they'd once been.

"They took your eyes…"

"They stole my first sight, not my second." Her lips, thin and pale, trembled. "There are places where I can still see."

"You knew I was coming?"

The witch cocked her head oddly to the side, as if she'd heard something off in the distance. "I *always* know."

"Julia," I said.

"Julia," she whispered. "*Julia…*"

"Is she here?"

"Not anymore."

"They let her leave?"

The witch gave no answer.

"Is she alive?" I pressed.

"She still lives."

Relief washed over me. "Did they hurt her?"

"No more than they've hurt you. But she disarmed them. Not with force, but tenderness. She mothered them. She was *kind*, listened to their childish nonsense with patience and grace, told them stories of the Promised Land, said one day she'd be back for them. They believed her. They think she's some sort of fairy godmother. And so, they set her free."

Julia. Only Julia.

"And those they don't set free wind up with their heads on a spike, is that it?"

"You've no idea what they're capable of, Dreamcatcher. There have been strangers that begged for such a fate, who would've gladly chosen decapitation over what was done to them. Few receive such mercies. Fewer still ever leave this place." Chthonia stood perfectly still, the light from the fire flickering across her horrible eyeless face. "Alive or otherwise…"

I tried to stand again but my legs still weren't cooperating.

"You are in great pain."

"You think? I've taken beatings before."

"Yes…" The witch looked back over her shoulder at the fire and held a hand out toward the flames, as if she planned to press her palm into them. "But that's not the pain I speak of, rather that which goes deep into your core, that which knows how to break you like no other. Battered bodies and broken bones heal with time and care. This is a deeper agony, a different kind of pain. Isn't that right, Dreamcatcher?"

There seemed little reason to answer, so I didn't.

The old woman smiled. The few teeth left in her head were rotten, black and fizzing with blood and disease. "Such delicious misery…such pure, ruthless torture…"

"I have to get out of here," I told her. "One way or another, you understand? You help me, I'll help you."

"There is no help for me."

"Help me get out of this place and I'll see that you get out too."

"An old blind woman, alone, out there, in that madness?" She brought her mangled hands to her face. "Even *my* magic has limits, Dreamcatcher."

"I don't kill children," I told her.

"But…"

"But I'll slaughter every single one of them if I have to."

The old hag cackled, the gurgling in her lungs now rattling in her chest. "And they call it *love*," she said. "Nothing spills more blood or topples more kingdoms. Powerful as it is, hatred pales in comparison."

"I have to find her."

"So you say."

"Am I close?"

She turned back to the fire.

"Answer me, witch. Am I close?"

"Closer than you think. But your journey is far from over."

I managed to stand, though my legs were shaking and I was

still light-headed. Staggering, I found my way to the table and dropped down into one of the chairs, out of breath and sore.

Chthonia gathered a tin cup from the mantel of the fireplace and swept it through the flames the way one might draw water from a well. Whispering her spells and prayers, she moved her free hand over the cup. Smoke rose from it, then spiraled away. Turning, she held the cup out for me with a shaking hand.

I took it, felt the heat from within and looked inside. It was filled with a clear liquid.

"Drink," she said. "It will heal you."

"What is this? I need water."

"What good would water do your kind? Water cleanses. *Fire* is what you require. Only fire heals." She returned to the flames and muttered more spells. The fire responded, flashing brighter and stronger as her laughter screeched all around us.

I had no choice but to trust her, so I drank the concoction, swallowing it down in a single gulp. A bitter taste filled my mouth and a burning sensation tore down along my throat and into my abdomen with such violence I found myself doubled over and sliding from the chair.

I dropped to the floor, holding my midsection and trying to draw breath. "What have you done to me?"

I gasped, choking on the words, the pain growing so severe all my other injuries were forgotten.

"Through destruction," Chthonia gurgled, "rebirth…"

* * *

Things move in ways I do not understand. The light—our light—artificial or even natural as a flame—bends and dances, creeping along the walls and floors and ceiling. A thief, it sneaks closer, slithering like a snake, wrapping around me slowly, coiling and tightening and making everything wrong, impossible, out of sync.

Everything spins and tilts and sways, bouncing slowly and steadily, eerily…

And then the sky, red as the flames climbing the walls, flickers up

from the bottom of my eyes and rolls overhead, clouds dark and men-
acing in all that brilliantly angry crimson, they move at speeds un-
like any I have seen before, soaring above an endless stretch of empty
highway.

Stumbling, I move down the middle of the road, but I can bare-
ly stand, much less walk. The world is not dark but a dull gray, not
without light and yet, not of the light.

I see no one, nothing, only empty expanses of desert and wasteland.

But I am not alone.

Something whispers to me and I stagger, turning to find it. In the
distance, the witch stands in the center of the highway, arms out-
stretched in mock crucifixion. Her cackling laughter, so hideous and
evil, drifts slowly closer. Flames burn from her twisted fingertips, but
she seems to revel in it, smiling as she holds them up before what
should be her eyes.

I drop to my knees.

Sounds…strange clicking sounds…like a thousand insects scurry-
ing toward me…

No, not insects…children, it's the children, walking in unison
along the paved road, emerging over the horizon behind the witch
and taking up position on either side of her. Except for the dark pools
that are their eyes, they've all turned a horrifying shade of white, too
pale to still be alive. Yet there they are. Have they covered themselves
in some sort of powder or paint?

Canned laughter echoes from the outskirts of my hearing, barely
audible over the steady whisper of a strengthening wind.

The world moves like liquid, thick gelatinous liquid.

Like slowly congealing blood…

"Can you hear me?" Julia asks from nowhere and everywhere, her
voice urgent and frightened. "Can you hear me?"

I close my eyes. I don't want to see anymore. I cover my ears with
my hands so I won't have to hear anything either, but I can feel this
strange netherworld unfurling all around me.

"Open your eyes, Dreamcatcher," someone whispers, this time the
witch. She whispers in my ear, her breath hot and fetid, lips brush-
ing against me, cold and dead. "You're a man of great power, but

that power is leaving you. It's dying in you, slowly, gradually, like the darkness you hide yourself in, like the life in the lost souls you've hunted down and butchered. What you don't know is that you've come to set us both free. So open your eyes, Dreamcatcher. Open your eyes and see..."

I do.

The woman she once was...or is it Julia...stands before me. I cannot be certain because her long dark hair hangs in her face, blocking it, and tattered sheets cover her body as she shuffles closer. Gone is the highway, and I am back in the hut, near the fire now, kneeling and staring into it as the woman slithers around behind me, moving like a serpent, her breath hissing in long exhales that stoke the fire.

I can hear nothing but her horrible hissing, the crackling flames and my own labored breath. I want to turn and look at her, to see who she is, who she really is, but I cannot take my eyes from the fire. There are things within it that demand my attention. Evil things... horrible things...deadly things...

"Am I...awake?" I ask, the words slurred and distant and falling from my mouth without my approval.

"It is your god that sleeps," she tells me, "while you lie awake, writhing in agony."

The witch, fooling me, trying to convince me she's something other than the horrible old hag she truly is. A shape-shifter and sorcerer, I cannot allow myself to believe her, even as she wraps her arms around me, leans closer and puts her lips against the side of my throat.

"Go," she whispers. "Go to the fire."

I lean closer, feel the heat against my face and neck, my chest. In the distance, somewhere out there in this godforsaken village of children, a bell tolls eerily in the night, once...again...and again... and strange sounds fill my head, like the ethereal cries of some ancient giant creature, its wailing song both unsettling and somehow peaceful.

I fall forward, into the flames, eyes wide open.

And I burn.

Through the flames, the witch dances, spinning and nude, younger now and beautiful, she throws her head back and through my burning eyes, I see hers as they were before they were stolen. And in those beautifully terrifying eyes, a night sky lives and breathes, lording over a throng of children standing alongside a giant bonfire. I am among them, bound, shackled and on my knees, battered and barely conscious as they stand and stare in silent judgment.

I call Julia's name, scream it as long and loud as I can.

Their dirty pale faces come closer, their tiny fingers pulling and prodding and poking me, shaking me and pushing and shoving, they—they're killing me, they—they're tearing me apart and closing over me so that I can no longer see the fire or hear anything but their hideous cries and the sound of my flesh being torn from the bone.

And then there are only my screams, of horror and agony, surrender and death. Destruction…and rebirth…

* * *

Startled, I came awake certain the witch's diseased fingers were reaching out of the darkness for me. But it was only the gnarled branches of that old tree. I found myself sitting on the ground, my back against the car. On a distant ridge overlooking the valley below, fires burned, and a crowd of children stood side-by-side along its edge, still as statues in the night. I reached for my shotgun, but the holster was empty. As I forced myself to my feet, ignoring the pain in my leg and back, I saw the weapon had been left on the ground next to me. By the time I scooped it up, Chael and Amy had broken free of the others and were walking toward me.

Confused and disoriented, I tried to clear my head and make sense of what was happening, what had happened, but everything was murky. Rather than return my shotgun to its holster, I held it down against my thigh.

Chael carried a torch, his rifle slung casually over his shoulder, while Amy carried with both hands an object wrapped in white gauze. Once they'd gotten close enough for me to see the whites of their eyes, they stopped. Amy smiled at me warmly, innocently. Even she was insane.

"Julia," the boy said. "She's coming back for us."

"Yes," I lied.

"I'm not asking. I'm telling you."

"I understand."

"You understand nothing. You're just a machine that kills when it's told to. But Julia understands. Julia cares, and she's coming back for us." He held the torch a bit higher and took a closer look at me. "And because she loves you, like she loves us, we've decided to let you live. We've decided to let you go to her."

I stood there, unsure of what to say.

"Chthonia, the witch, she showed us things," he added.

"What kind of things?"

"The future," he said, as if this should've been obvious. "Some think she was lying so we'd let you go and set her free." His eyes turned colder. "But I know the truth. She brought you here with her magic, so you could go to Julia and protect her on her journey to the Promised Land. Then she'll come back for us. Chthonia brought you here to save us all."

I nodded, pretending I had some idea as to what the hell he was babbling about.

"So I'm letting you go," Chael said, motioning to Amy.

Amy took the material covering the thing in her arms and pulled it free.

As it spiraled down to the ground in a graceful pirouette, I realized it was a sheer veil, the same one the witch had worn.

"This is for you," Amy said in her sweet little voice, hands clutching either side of Chthonia's severed head by its blood-soaked hair, struggling to hold it up before her with all the strength her tiny body could muster.

Those aren't children.

The eyeless face of the witch swayed in the night, the flames from the torch lapping at it as if to lick the blood free of its ravaged flesh.

"Give it to Julia," Chael commanded. "It proves she's the only one we worship now. Only her magic is what matters."

When I didn't take it, the boy nodded to Amy and she let it go. The head fell and bounced, rolled closer to me, then lay still.

What you don't know is that you've come to set us both free...

Chael took Amy by the hand, turned, and together, they walked back toward the others. The little girl looked back long enough to smile at me once more and offer a quick wave.

I fumbled around in my coat pocket until I'd found my cigarettes, then rolled one into the corner of my mouth and greedily drew on it. After a few deep drags, I went to the car, found my leather gloves and pulled them on.

Grabbing the head by the stringy, bloody hair, I hoisted it up, walked around to the rear of the car, popped the trunk and tossed it inside. It landed with a dull thud, spraying the underside with blood and tissue.

You are violence, Dreamcatcher, why should such things bother your kind?

With only the dim light from the trunk, I couldn't see much, but I stared down at what remained of Chthonia for a long while anyway. I still didn't fully understand what had happened and probably never would, but none of that concerned me now.

I was battered and hobbled, but alive. And at least for now, so was Julia.

Nothing else mattered.

I slammed closed the trunk, flicked my cigarette into the night, then slid behind the wheel and headed for the highway.

PART TWO

"The terminal point of addiction is damnation."
—W.H. Auden

CHAPTER TWELVE

I don't know how long I'd been driving. The road kept coming and the night seemed to last forever. Headlights cut the darkness, and the old girl kept rocketing along, but more than once she sputtered, bucked and threatened to stall out. There wasn't much life left in either one of us, apparently. I was hungry, tired and thirsty, and although when I'd left the city I'd thrown a few bottles of water in the trunk, they were long gone now. My mouth was ash dry, my stomach was tearing itself apart and I was weak and getting weaker. At a minimum I needed to find some water, and soon.

The dash lights blinked, drawing my attention to the gauges. I was almost out of gas. I wondered how much longer I'd have. In the last few hours I hadn't seen a single building or other living thing, only darkness and endless highway. Eventually I'd end up walking, and who knew what was out there? We'd all heard the stories about the marauders that supposedly traveled these outlands, robbing, raping and killing anyone foolish enough to be out in this wilderness in the first place, ultra-violent crazies so far gone, unreliable and volatile they were even beyond nightmare work. Banished to the outlands and long forgotten, they were also rumored to be cannibals. Because there were no animals out here, no other real sources of food, they consumed the flesh of others, including their own kind. Word was such practices made them even crazier. Maybe those were rumors, stories spun from the minds of those with nothing better to do. I had no way of knowing for sure, but something told me when the car died and I was on foot, it'd only be a matter of time before I had my answers.

You're just a machine that kills when it's told to.

That little punk's words kept coming back to me, replaying in my head no matter how many times I tried to ignore them and focus on something else. To him, I was no different than the savages that allegedly ran free in these outlands, a bloodthirsty killer that lived for chaos and cruelty and violence. What he and others didn't understand was that for most Dreamcatchers, it was just a job. There were those who enjoyed the killing, but I'd never been one of them. I didn't feel anything one way or the other, although I always found it easier if they fought back. The harder they fought the more justified my actions seemed. Regardless, often, once it was done, I felt sorrow for having been given such a task, and sometimes felt sorry for the runner as well. But I had a job to do, and I did it. Judgment had nothing to do with me or my duty; that was for others. I came later, an executioner carrying out orders from those more important and powerful than I'd ever be. For me, it was get the job done, then go home and forget it as best I could. If that meant drinking or drugs or sex or whatever else, so be it. We all had to get through the night and sleep the day as best we could.

For some reason, memories of a particular runner came to me then, one that had always bothered me more than the others. A woman, she couldn't have been more than twenty or so, had run but didn't get far. I cornered her on a tram car but couldn't risk firing a weapon because the car was full. We rode on that tram for what seemed forever, her standing there holding on to a rail and me near the doors, my hand in my coat pocket and clutching the gun I'd later use to end her existence in this world. She never once pleaded for her life, never cried or even said a word, never even fought back or tried to stop me or save herself in any way, she just stared at me with these big blue eyes, stared like she knew something I didn't, and maybe she did.

Maybe that young girl knew a lot of things I didn't.

For nearly an hour we stayed on the tram as it moved through the city, stopping now and then to let off passengers or take on new ones. And finally, when it reached the end of the line and we were the only two left in the car, I walked over to her, took out my revolver and told her I needed her to come in with me.

She shook her head no but she never took her eyes from me.

I asked her again; and again, she shook her head.

I shot her in the neck and down she went. She lay there on the floor of the tram car, eyes wide with shock and a hand pressed uselessly against the wound as her body began to convulse. She never made a sound. I sat on the nearest bench, lit a cigarette and watched her bleed out. Then I called it in, hit a bar, had as many drinks as I could stand and went home to Julia.

"Why do they make me do it?" I asked her later that night, as we lay in a tangle of cool sheets and sweaty flesh.

"They don't have to make you," Julia said. "They give the order and you obey."

I never told her that's not what I'd meant. I was referring to the runners.

So much blood, so much death…

Maybe we'd all sold our souls to the darkness. Maybe that's why we were here.

But why? For what? I'd always wondered if that young woman even knew why she was running, or where the hell she thought she was running to. Did it even matter?

None of it made any goddamn sense. It never had.

Don't worry, I heard Lenore's voice say in my mind, *the night loves her children.*

"This isn't love," I muttered.

We're parlor tricks...rumors whispered in the rain...in darkness...

Maybe Gideon was smarter than any of us, locked away with her books.

I forced everything from my mind, focused on the road, and drove into the night.

Sometime later, the earliest hints of dawn began to break over the horizon, partially illuminating the road ahead, beyond the headlights, and it was then that I realized there *was* no road ahead. The highway was coming to an end.

I slowed the car and it coughed, sputtered and stalled. Coasting, I eased my foot onto the brake and slowly pulled over. Perhaps fifty yards or so ahead, the highway simply stopped and became dirt. But there was something more. My headlights settled on another car parked at an odd angle at the edge of the road. It looked like it had skidded into a sideways position and been left there. Black smoke billowed from beneath the hood. Whatever had happened here hadn't taken place that long ago.

I checked my mirrors and looked out as far as I could see. Nothing. The grass was higher here, but the ground was flat and open. I grabbed my shotgun, made sure it was loaded, and then climbed from the car, ignoring the pain ravaging me from head to toe.

Keeping an eye on my surroundings and using the headlights to guide me, I walked slowly toward the smoking vehicle, the shotgun in hand. By the time I'd gotten within twenty feet of it, I recognized the car as the black rocket of a sports sedan Dingo drove. They'd sent him for Julia, and for me, like Eddie said they eventually would. That meant he'd likely found Eddie's body, which also meant HQ now knew Eddie was dead too, and I'd been the one that killed her. That meant others were coming too. I'd have had zero chance with both Eddie and Dingo on my case, but Dingo alone wasn't good enough to take me down by himself, and they all knew it. With Eddie terminated, there was no question Cap would pull all the stops and send half the goddamn department after me. Apparently Dingo had missed my car parked off-road under that old tree and went right by, unaware that I was no longer on the road ahead of him but had been taken by the children instead. He'd wound up here, at the literal end of the road. Now there was no sign of him, at least not yet.

I noticed something on the highway between the car and myself. A machete lay in the middle of the road. I crouched down, picked it up. Dingo carried this, he was a blade guy, liked to use knives whenever he could, and was known to favor machetes over guns. But despite the acrid odor of heavy black smoke pouring from the hood of his car, the smell of gunpowder lingered in the air as well. Weapons had been fired here, and recently, which meant Dingo had been outnumbered and gone to his gun out of necessity.

For a moment, I stayed where I was and listened to what remained of the night.

A light breeze blew through the open expanse of flatlands but otherwise the slowly dying darkness was quiet. I stood up and moved closer to Dingo's car. No one inside, but a duffel bag likely used to carry an arsenal of weapons sat on the seat, torn open and empty now, a few bullets scattered about.

As I rounded the front of the vehicle, I saw a smear of blood along the road in front of the car. A wide swath, it had clearly come from a horrific wound. I stepped around it and onto the side of the road.

Dawn was breaking, it was time to sleep.

But I wasn't alone out here.

I looked back at the road. A pair of skid marks painted a path, showing where Dingo's car had screeched to a stop. He'd been ambushed, forced from the road. I walked back toward the marks and noticed a second set, these much thinner. They appeared in the center of the highway, then turned and abruptly stopped.

And then there came a deep growling sound. In the distance, drawing closer. I looked down the stretch of highway from which I'd come, and although the light was stronger now, it still wasn't sufficient for me to see what was coming. But I knew that sound, and the tracks here gave it away. A motorcycle was headed right for me. For the briefest moment I pictured Falcon Eddie flying toward me on her giant silver chopper. But this was something different, something worse.

A horrible burst of maniacal laughter followed the sound of heavy footfalls from the other side of the road. I spun and saw several dark forms charging toward me. Dressed entirely in black, they were hard to discern in the limited light, but I knew what they were. The stories were true.

They attacked from the side while another came straight at me down the highway on a battered black motorcycle, controlling the bike with one hand and swinging an enormous heavy chain in the air with the other. They looked like the crazies they were, their hair either shaved off or into Mohawks, faces littered with tattoos of odd symbols and smeared with war paint, mouths still wet with Dingo's flesh and blood, their eyes diseased, demented and wild.

I slid between the vehicles, out of the way of the oncoming motorcycle, then leveled my shotgun and fired at the crazies charging on foot, pumped, and fired again.

The marauder closest, a short but powerful-looking bald man leading the charge and screaming like a banshee, was blown backward off his feet as his midsection exploded in a burst of blood and tissue.

As he fell away, I dropped the now-empty shotgun and met the next in line with a swing of the machete. With a sickening sound, it struck him in the side of the neck, above the shoulder, but didn't even slow him.

The hatchet in his hand swept past my face, barely missing me as I arched my back in an attempt to get out of the way. As I yanked the machete free, ribbons of blood flew into the air. I turned, gripping the machete with both hands, and swung it up and around, bringing the blade down across his arm and severing it at the elbow. The limb fell at our feet, the hand still clutching the ax, and while the man howled and staggered about in shock, glaring at the bloody, stringy stump that was now his arm, I dropped into a crouch and slammed the machete up into his gut. Standing, and again using both hands, I brought the blade with me, drawing it higher and up into his chest, tearing everything in its path as it went.

Vomiting blood and bile, he gagged and dropped to his knees, but the others were on me now, punching and kicking and knocking me to the ground. I rolled away as best as I could. One of them swung a huge mallet again and again, crashing it against the ground, missing me several times by mere inches. I came to a stop once I reached the dirt, and rolled onto my back. By then I'd managed to pull the revolver free of my coat and was already firing.

The first shot hit the man with the mallet directly in the forehead. He fell, but two more took his place. I fired the remaining five bullets in rapid succession. Two rounds missed, one took down another attacker, hitting him in the eye and blowing out a good chunk of the back of his skull, and the other two hit the last of them, littering his torso with wounds.

I scrambled to my feet. The man was badly wounded but still attempting to get to his feet, so I kicked him in the side of the head. Once he was on his back, I found the severed arm of his cohort, pried the ax from its dead fingers, then returned and slammed it down into his skull, until he stopped moving and the top of his head had become a bloody, frothy mess.

Stumbling away, I looked to the road. This wasn't over yet. The motorcycle had turned and was headed back for me a second time. Still clutching the bloody ax, I readied myself.

The motorcycle closed on me faster than I thought possible, blowing by as the driver screamed like the madman he was. The chain flew in the air, this time hitting me in the shoulder with such force it knocked me off my feet and sent me sprawling back into the dirt. Pain exploded through my shoulder, shooting up into my neck and down the length of my arm into my hand. A tingling sensation followed and my arm went limp.

I got to my knees in time to see him coming back around.

My arm dangling dead at my side, I managed to get back to my feet. With my good arm, I timed it, waiting as if I'd resigned myself to being executed by him on this pass. But when he was close enough, I threw the ax directly at his head.

He was so close I could see his eyes widening in realization: the blade spinning through the air was not going to miss. At his speed there was no way he could stop, so he did the only thing he could do, which was to ditch the bike and throw himself off the back of it before the ax buried itself in his face.

He toppled onto the highway and bounced, tumbling about as the motorcycle crashed onto its side and skidded away along with him. Spraying the road with debris, both motorcycle and rider finally came to a stop a distance away.

The bike was still running, but the man, lying in the fetal position on the pavement a few feet from it, wasn't moving. I looked around to make sure there weren't any more of them. The road and flatlands were empty and still. The night was almost gone.

Gathering up my revolver and shotgun with my good arm, I staggered down the road toward the fallen rider. When I got there, I realized he was in bad shape and broken up, but alive. He looked up at me with his crazy eyes and laughed. Then he made a strange sucking sound, as if he were trying to taste me, or perhaps the remnants on his lips of what had once been Dingo.

He wasn't going anywhere ever again, and we both knew it.

There was no way Julia could've survived an attack from these madmen, so all I could hope was that she'd been lucky and passed through here unnoticed.

Or maybe she didn't need luck. Maybe something greater guided and protected her, and she was everything those sad and forgotten children believed she was.

I was beginning to wonder.

The rider snarled at me and said something unintelligible, bringing me back.

It wasn't easy, but I managed to reload the shotgun with one hand.

Then I spattered his head all over the pavement and walked back to my car.

My ride was as dead as the bloody bodies all around me. I'd be walking from now on. I fell back against it like the old friend it was and tried to collect myself, but wasn't sure how much more I could take. I still couldn't feel or move my arm, and the rest of my body was giving out too. Exhausted, hungry, drained and injured, I could barely think straight. For the first time since I was a child, or what I remembered to be my childhood anyway, I felt like crying, letting go and allowing every scrap of emotion to flow from me like water.

I smoked a couple cigarettes instead. After cleaning the machete off on one of their coats, I slid it into my belt, then searched the bodies for anything I could use. I came up empty, but when I searched the motorcycle, I found a full canteen in its saddlebag. After smelling and tasting a drop from my fingertip, I determined it was only water and seemed safe to drink. I took a long pull and felt almost immediately revitalized.

But the feeling was short-lived.

The breeze picked up, cold and harsh. In the growing light, beyond the edge of the highway and in the distance, a range of mountains dominated the horizon. I needed to sleep, but I needed Julia more, and while I'd handled this band of marauders, there were almost certainly many more in the area. The only sign of Dingo was the blood on the road, so it was likely a larger group had taken him down, brought his body to some nearby camp where he was slaughtered and eaten, and then this smaller patrol had returned to the scene to scavenge whatever else they could use. Evidently I'd come upon Dingo's car at the worst possible time, and now that none of these crazies would be returning to their brood, sooner than later, others would come looking for them. I had to put as much distance between me and this bloody scene as quickly as possible.

I pictured Julia out here all alone, traversing the vast stretch of empty flatland leading to the horizon. If she'd made it this far, there was nowhere else to go, no other direction that made sense, so with what little resolve and strength I had left, I walked toward those mountains.

And whatever awaited me on the other side.

CHAPTER THIRTEEN

Hobbled with my leg injury and with one arm all but useless, I walked on, trying not to think about the pain and exhaustion, and ignoring the quiet voice in my head that kept insisting I should stop, lie down for a while, and sleep. The day had come, but here, in the mountains, things were different. By the time I'd reached the base of the range, it had begun to snow. I'd seen snow before, of course, in the city, though out here it was more ominous. It clouded the sky and left the world in neither the darkness I was used to nor the total daylight forbidden to my kind. Instead, I found myself wandering through a strange chasm between the two, and the higher into the mountains I climbed, the heavier the snow became and the lower the temperature dropped.

I cursed myself for not taking some of the marauders' coats, they'd have come in handy for extra insulation and warmth, but I'd had no idea it would be snowing here, much less to this degree. Besides, in my decrepit state, I could barely carry my own things. For Christ's sake, I could scarcely walk. And it was getting worse.

My breath churned from my lungs in living clouds, mixed with the blowing snow and increasingly heavy winds. The snow became deeper. I pressed on.

There was nothing here but frozen ground, uneven terrain, snow and ice. I felt like the last living thing in this terrible world of ours. Eventually, I found a jutting section of rock overhanging the entrance to a small cave. I ducked inside to find a clear and empty space that looked to have at one point been part of a larger cave system. Rocks had fallen and slid down from above long ago, blocking the entrance from the rest. What remained was a cramped space not even high enough for me to stand in and barely deep enough to accommodate me. But it was shelter from the wind and snow, if not the cold. From hands and knees, I collapsed onto my side, out of breath and racked with pain, I lay there, curled up into myself and doing my best to stay warm.

I slept. Though I couldn't be sure how long I was out, it seemed both a long time and not nearly enough, as I came awake coughing and shivering violently. My eyes took a while to focus, and at first I was unsure of where I was. When I remembered, I pushed myself upright as far as I could without hitting my head on the rocky ceiling above me, and looked out at the storm.

But there was no storm. I could hear it, but a wall of snow now blocked the entrance I'd crawled through. Despite the pain, I managed to maneuver myself onto my back, and kicked the snow out with my boots. It was a crusty and frozen skin that fell away easily, and I was immediately met with a stinging gust of wind and a burst of fresh snowflakes blowing in from outside.

I took a sip of water from the canteen, then tried to move my damaged arm. I could flex my fingers and feel my hand; that was about it. The arm itself was still dead, though a pulsing pain pounded steadily in my shoulder. My injured leg was stiff and sore, but at least I was able to bend my knee without unbearable pain.

I crawled out of the cave and into the darkness. I lay there a moment, and considered letting the storm take me. I was so goddamn tired I didn't want to fight anymore. I wanted to sleep, but I knew if I did now, I'd freeze to death out here, so I pushed myself to my feet, brushed the excess snow from my body and looked around as best I could. In the dark and such extreme cold, it was difficult to tell where my breath ended and the garlands of snow falling all around me began.

Teeth chattering, I hobbled through the snow, hopeful I'd continued in the same direction as before. Within minutes my eyes were crusted with snow and ice and I was shivering so violently I was having trouble controlling my body.

Hugging myself tight, I tucked chin to chest and pushed on. I was walking uphill at a steeper angle than before, and with my bad leg it was difficult to get enough push to drive myself through the deep snow at such an incline. But somehow I managed to stagger forward into this hell of ice and snow.

As the wind cut through me like a razor, I grimaced as another series of violent shivers throttled me. As I reached up to paw snow from my frost-covered face, I felt the ground give way beneath me. Falling. I was falling through the darkness and snow.

I landed hard on my back and lay there motionless, weak and in pain.

Coughing, I watched the flakes descending on me, blowing all about, and this time wasn't sure I could get back up. I struggled for breath, was finally able to draw some, then coughed again and without thinking about it, was suddenly rolling over onto my hands and knees.

Get up. Get up or you'll die here. You'll fall asleep and die here.

I got back to my feet.

Trying to find my bearings in the curtains of snow, all I knew for sure was that I'd somehow made it to the other side of the incline, as the ground pitched sharply downward now.

I swayed with the wind, nearly collapsed but remained up-right.

Trudging forward, my feet sunk deeper into the snow as I went, and I had the sensation that at any moment I might pitch forward and tumble helplessly down the steep mountainside and into the darkness.

Defiantly, I pushed deeper into the tempest.

Trapped in the storm, time lost all meaning. I might've been lumbering through the snow for hours or moments, I could no longer be sure. What I did know was that my lungs had begun to burn and ache, my heart was hammering my chest and my eyes stung so badly I could only open them in brief intervals before they began to tear and close again on their own.

Although my lips were badly cracked and my exposed flesh was burned and raw, most of the sensation in my body was gone. The only real pain I still felt was a sharp throbbing beneath my skull and deep inside my head. Fear was the only thing that kept me going, because I knew if I fell now, I'd never be able to get back up and the storm would take me.

Suddenly the wind changed, not in velocity, but in the way it sounded. By rote, I kept moving, staggering forward, but there was something more now. I could hear it, somewhere out there in the night, carried on this frozen wind.

Singing, the most beautiful singing I'd ever heard. Like the chanting of angels, if such things existed, ever had or ever could, it had an undeniably ethereal quality, and I found myself drawn to it. But I couldn't figure out exactly where it was coming from. It might've been behind me but could've emanated from the darkness ahead of me. It was as if the voices were born of the night and snow, swirling around with those endless flakes of ice bursting and dancing in the darkness.

I reached out a shaking hand, pushing it up into the air as if to grab hold of the beautiful sound. There seemed no end or beginning to the storm, to the night or even to me. The singing grew louder and even more beautiful.

Within the darkness, I thought I saw something. Blinking

and wiping my eyes, I stumbled forward, closer to it, but it still seemed the same distance away. Two, three, perhaps more, dark figures, silhouettes barely discernible in the night, stood in a row, watching me.

I began to laugh, though I had no idea why.

Was I hallucinating? Was my mind slowly dying and playing tricks on me?

An odd sensation came over me, and it wasn't until I'd hit the snow that I realized I'd dropped to my knees. Swaying, my eyes barely open, I strained to see through the storm. But the figures were gone, and instead, something else caught my attention.

In the flakes, written on them, was something more…

A palace, unlike anything I'd ever seen or even imagined, appeared before me in the distance, emerging from the walls of snow like a mirage. Made entirely of ice and crystals, mirrors and dreams, it was the most beautiful and terrifying thing I'd ever seen.

I fell forward, flopping onto my belly in the snow. Lying there on my stomach, I felt my body begin to convulse and seize. I crawled forward, toward that mysterious palace in the ice, digging my hands into the blankets of snow and pulling myself closer.

Light…Light…There's a light, I…I see a light…

Within the darkness, it emanated from the crystal palace of ice and dreams. I squinted through the snow and tried to focus on it, reaching out for it with my good arm, but then a sudden burst of heavy snow engulfed me, and everything vanished in the whiteout.

All that remained was the bitter cold, and the sound of those Heavenly chants.

* * *

When I awakened, although I was warm, the only thing I heard was a muffled, though steady and howling wind. My eyes opened but sight came to me gradually, painfully, my eyelids flaking and crackling free as I blinked. Blood, ice or both slid along my cheeks. As my vision slowly returned, I understood why the wind sounded distant. It was outside, beyond the walls of the room in which I found myself.

Lying on my back in a bed of sorts, I was covered with thick animal furs for blankets, in a small though magnificent room of crystals, ice and mirrors.

And I was not alone.

Three figures stood just beyond the foot of my bed, shrouded in long, dark hooded robes. I could not see their faces, and their hands were tucked into the wide sleeves of their robes. I swallowed, gagged and coughed a moment, the sound ricocheting along the beautiful and glistening walls. I struggled to bring the beings before me into better focus.

"Where am I?" I asked, my voice raw, weak and unfamiliar.

The strange hooded figures offered no response.

"Who are you?"

Again, there was no reply.

"Am I...*alive*?" I bit my lip in the hopes of preventing it from trembling.

Things moved along the mirrors and in the reflections of the crystals and ice. The dreams and nightmares of the living and dead, playing out before me, here, in this strange little room, and beyond, in the hallways of glass and ice I could now make out behind my shrouded hosts.

"Julia," I gasped. "*Julia...*"

The figures turned in unison, and shuffled out of the room.

"Wait," I said, sitting up. The furs slid down, and I realized I was nude. My shoulder and arm were hideously bruised from the chain that had struck me, but I could feel and move both again, albeit with soreness, and I was clean, my other wounds tended to. Had they *bathed* me?

Light-headed, I gathered one of the furs around me and climbed out of bed, my bare feet cold against a floor of ice. My clothes were folded neatly on an ornate chair of glass in the corner, my boots standing next to it. Hurriedly, I dressed, watching the dreams play out before me in the mirrors. What was this palace of dreams, of ice and glass and crystal? Who were these beings that saved me, who ironically enough, looked like monks? I listened. No sound but for the wind outside. This was a place of silence, like a monastery or a church. Although I'd never set foot in either one, I knew of such things, and had once terminated a runner on the steps of an old church in the bowels of the city. But none of that mattered now. This place was unlike any other.

Once dressed, I checked my coat before pulling it on, but could not locate any of my weapons. A quick look around the small room turned up nothing. I'd always felt incomplete without my weapons, but for some reason in this strange place I did not.

While neither my legs nor my balance were back to normal, they were much better, and I was able to walk through the open doorway and into the hall without fear of collapsing.

Mirrors lined the walls, ceiling, even the floor. And on those mirrors all the dreams and nightmares one could imagine silently played continuously, like an endless loop of film. The hallway was long and narrow, a house of mirrors and sparkling crystal, and at the end it branched off into several additional hallways.

Disoriented, I was unsure of which path to take, so I hesitated and watched the stories unfolding all around me. And then at the end of one hallway, I noticed something that set it apart from the others. A room, and in that room a figure, sitting at a table, its back to me.

The moment I saw it, the strange ethereal chanting I'd heard out in the storm resumed, barely audible but unmistakable. It stirred something deep within me, and the closer I got to the room at the end of the hallway the stronger it became. I continued toward it, the heels of my boots clicking along the glass, and soon realized that the person sitting at the table was an old man. His back was to me, but I could see he was dressed in moccasin slippers and a silk robe with flannel pajamas beneath. His hair was white as talcum powder and very thin on top, his balding head pale and littered with sizable brown age spots. The room, which was otherwise empty, was constructed entirely of glistening ice.

With equal parts fascination and fear, I stepped into the room.

If the old man noticed me, he gave no indication, so I moved around the side of the table for a better look at him. He was just sitting there, his sad eyes staring straight ahead, this impossibly ancient man, face hollow and ravaged with age and wrinkles, his body frail and thin. The chanting grew louder, as did the howling wind beyond the walls of this curious place. I reached out for the old man, cautiously, and when my hand came to rest on his bony shoulder, he tried to slowly turn and look at me, but his neck appeared too stiff to allow it, so his eyes slid toward me instead. He seemed to be struggling to breathe, his aged lungs unable to draw anything but wheezing, erratic gulps of air. His eyes narrowed, as if he were losing sight of me, then his face twisted into a strange expression of disbelief, made all the more powerful and profound because I knew in that moment of absolute madness, my expression was no different.

The old man was me.

And I was he.

"*Can you hear me?*"

Julia's voice, from somewhere close by, echoed through the room and beyond, emanating from deep within this chamber of ice and dreams.

"*Can you hear me?*" she asked again, urgently this time. "*Can you hear me?*"

As the palace began to quake, and the ice cracked and crumbled all around us, the endless dreams, nightmares and players closed on me, so many faces and scenarios exploding across the walls and ceilings and floors, distorted and ghoulish flashes in a demented funhouse of mirrors. I stumbled over to the front of the table, reached out and cupped the old man's face—my face—in my hands. I wanted to will away our pain, but all I saw in those sad eyes was confusion and terror.

The violent rumbling and the din of shattering glass, ice and crystal grew worse, the cries of infinite dreams raining down on us, lethal as any act of violence I had ever committed.

With a thunderous roar, the world liquefied and became something else.

Alone in the room, sitting at the table, I looked down at my trembling hands, now old and stained with liver spots, the flesh thin and pale. I could barely draw breath. My vision was weak, my body fragile and hopelessly decrepit with age. Yet from somewhere within my muddled mind, there came a moment of lucidity, and I understood everything.

Everything…and nothing at all…

Gone were the dreams and the crystal palace of mirrors and ice. It was only a nondescript room now, a small black-and-white television sitting atop a rickety table in the corner. Rabbit ear antennas protruded from the top of the television, but the modest screen was fuzzy with wavy lines and crackling snow, the signal so distorted it was imperceptible. Strangely inexact sounds leaked from the television, gibberish that barely sounded human filtered through odd, rumbling, machine-like noises.

And then, unlike any I'd ever experienced before, came total…utter…silence.

"Can you hear me?"

"No," I whispered, the words slashing across my tongue like razors, "I can't."

CHAPTER FOURTEEN

My gradual apocalypse in full bloom, the world twisted and surged into a fiery wasteland void of not only the dreams that for so long had defined it, but the merchants of those dreams, the performers within them who existed for the benefit of those in the light. What the hell was I then? What had I ever really been, a ghost, someone else's vague memory at the outskirts of a nightmare that plagued them in the dark, a whisper in the night, one more flame in a larger, all-encompassing fire raining down on the dark, misty, dirty streets of Babylon?

Yet it was not fire that fell from the dark skies in my mind at all. It was blood.

A liquid sky of blood, spraying down onto us like the gruesome rain it was.

Tangled together, our mouths locked and our nude bodies slick and wet and covered in glistening crimson, we were almost beautiful, Julia and I, clinging to each other like the desperate and troubled lovers we'd always been. No words were spoken. No lies were told, no promises broken. Instead, I closed my eyes and allowed the blood and her touch to lead me to my sorrow… *through* my sorrow…

I could still taste her on my lips, on my tongue and the back of my throat as night gave way to the light. Was this really the end of the world? I couldn't be sure.

Something warm pulsed against my face. It felt like love, perhaps even safety.

As my eyes opened, they focused on the greenest, most beautiful grass I'd ever seen. An enormous field of it, slanted downward and continuing along flat ground for far as I could see, the tall beautiful stalks swayed gracefully in a gentle but steady warm wind. Lying at the edge of the field, legs curled up against me and my arms hugging myself tight, I turned my head, and squinting against the bright light, looked behind me.

In the distance, the mountains from which I'd come.

I rolled over onto my back, stretching out my arms and legs. The pain was still there but far weaker than before. My eyes blinked, tearing in the brightness and warmth washing down over me from above.

If we knew the sun, do you think we'd miss it?

Shielding my eyes with my forearm, I struggled to my feet. My legs were still a bit shaky but much stronger than before. My trench coat hung on me, long and heavy and hot. I reached for my leg. The holster and shotgun were gone. I checked my coat pockets. No revolver. Frantically, I searched the ground nearby but found nothing.

There's a place where birds sing in flight, gentle wind blows and the air is fresh and clean.

My weapons, I—I couldn't be without my weapons, I—

You can feel the sun as it warms you…

I looked to the sky. What was happening? Where the hell was I?

…and no one is afraid. At least not all the time.

"Fairy tales," I muttered.

146

No. It's true.

"Bedtime stories for the feeble-minded."

They stole it from us. And we let them.

Turning, I staggered down deeper into the field and onto flatter land. The farther I went, the stronger I felt and the faster I moved through the beautiful knee-high grass. The air here was different, crisp and new and filled with the aroma of salt, and as it filled my lungs it made me cough, expelling the phlegm cigarettes had left deep within them.

Soon, I'd broken into a full run, my coat, filthy and battered and flapping behind me like a cape, and in the sunshine and warmth, I ran like a child, effortlessly and with an abandon I had never before known.

Free. I felt absolutely free.

The field seemed to last forever, but so did my stamina and strength as I ran, farther and farther through the grass until I could see in the distance, a cliff where the field ended and turned to sand. I increased speed, galloping through the grass as fast as my legs would carry me.

When I eventually reached the massive cliff, I slowed to a walk and carefully approached the edge.

Below lay the most amazing thing I had ever laid eyes on.

A beach that went on on for miles, the sand a brilliant white, coconut palm trees scattered throughout, and beyond it, something I'd only seen before in movies or read about in books, something I hadn't believed really existed here. An ocean, with the clearest, cleanest water I'd ever seen, and above it, a bright blue cloudless sky that looked as if it stretched on for all eternity. In awe before this impossibly beautiful dream, I dropped and knelt before it like the breathtaking deity it was.

A heightened sense of awareness grabbed hold of me, and I remembered things. Ghostly voices and images flashed in my mind, reminding me of a life I'd lived before while offering glimpses of another existence that had only just begun. Was one life and the other death? One a waking life of clarity and the other a nightmare draped in troubled sleep? I couldn't be sure of anything anymore. All I knew for sure was that this light, this…*sunshine*…was different than any I'd ever known or experienced before. A creation of night, I'd never been comfortable outside my city of darkness, but in this light, and amidst such beauty, I didn't want to sleep, didn't feel as if I ought to sleep. Instead, I wanted to absorb it directly into me, drink it into my pores and feel its warmth transform me. But what would my metamorphosis entail? What would it transform me into?

As I watched the water, the waves rolling into the white sandy shore, I wondered if perhaps it had already happened and I was only now becoming aware of it. Emotions welled in me, and I wanted to weep, to kneel there on the edge of that cliff in the presence of these things I had for so long convinced myself were myths and cry like a child. But no tears came. Instead, I tilted back my head and let the warm breeze blow across my face and through my hair.

In time, I stood up and made my way carefully down the side of the cliffs to the beach below. The long white sands stretched into the sun, and the palm trees dotting the beach continued into the jungle beyond.

I'd begun to sweat profusely in the heat, so I pulled off my coat and let it drop to the sand, then rolled up my sleeves and looked around.

That's when I saw them, watching me from the edge of the jungle.

Instinctively, I reached for weapons that were no longer there. Maybe I wasn't changed after all. I'd know soon enough. So would they.

I counted six of them. They remained where they were, silent and unmoving, until I took a few steps toward them. Then they emerged from the jungle slowly but purposefully, this small and primitive-looking band of barefoot, bare-chested men with sinewy builds. Clad only in crude loincloths of battered animal hide, their hair was unkempt, their skin tanned a deep brown, and swaths of dark crimson streaks stained their faces like war paint, running from the bottoms of their eyes, across their cheeks and down across their chins. In their hands they carried makeshift clubs fashioned from stone, wood or bone. Even in this new world, the violence was never far, always lingering in the shadows, waiting for its chance. I didn't fear it—I never had—it was my game, and much as I no longer wanted to play, I was ready if need be. More ready than any of them, in fact, and I could only hope they realized that.

On the sand, they formed a single line across from me, but none of them spoke a word. They simply stared at me, as if trying to determine the level of threat I represented, so I maintained as relaxed a posture as possible, my expression neutral.

At this closer angle, I realized it wasn't red paint on their faces, but dried blood that had leaked from their eyes. More Night Sleepers, living in this sunshine and bright light of what I was sure they believed could only be their salvation.

Horrific, what the light did to them.

"Do you know who I am?" I asked.

They said nothing.

"I'm looking for Julia. My wife, Julia, I'm looking for her. Do you understand?"

One of them, a young man with wild and bushy dark hair barely contained by a headband of torn and faded cloth, glanced down at my coat, then back at me. His glassy eyes were intense but distant, ringed with crusted blood.

After a moment, he exchanged uncertain glances with the others.

"No weapons." I opened my hands and held out my arms to prove I wasn't concealing anything. "I'm not here to hurt anyone."

Had I wanted to, I could've disarmed one, then likely killed the rest. I could've turned this beautiful beach into a slaughterhouse before they even knew what hit them. I could've forced them to take me to Julia. I could've brought them so much pain they'd *beg* me for death. But at that point, unless my hand was forced, I wanted no part of violence anymore.

With the mesmerizing sound of ocean gently lapping nearby

shore, I recalled the dream Julia said I could not have had, that I *didn't* have. The dream of the beach, the people peering out at me from the jungle, all of it happening exactly as it had in my mind all those days ago. And as this realization took hold, I prepared myself for Julia's emergence from the jungle.

Instead, something else appeared from the cliffs behind me, surging through the air with a strange audible whine before slamming into the side of the first man's neck and exploding out the other side.

His eyes widened in disbelief and shock as he dropped his club and brought his hands to this throat. An arrow had been shot through his neck and was lodged there, glistening with blood in the brilliant sunshine.

CHAPTER FIFTEEN

I blinked the blood from my eyes, brought a hand to my face and wiped the rest away as the man collapsed to the sand and the others scattered, unsure of what was happening.

One of them came at me. I grabbed his hand, bent it at the wrist and gave it a savage twist, pulling him into me until I could get my other arm around his throat and face him outward, toward the cliffs. Using him as a shield, more arrows rained down from above. One, and then another, and then another still, being shot in rapid-fire succession.

Another man was struck in the center of his chest. He staggered back into the surf, then fell into the shallow ocean at the water's edge.

As I choked the man into unconsciousness, I squinted through the sun at the cliffs above, but the shooter was already gone, on the move toward the beach and jungle. I knew of only one person who used a bow, and if I was right, we were all dead.

I let the man go, laying him down in the sand.

The other three men had run back into the jungle, perhaps for cover, perhaps to find and bring back more of their kind.

I searched the immediate area and found a crude ax made of stone and bone one of them had dropped. Snatching it up, I tested the weight and action with a few quick swings, and then took off along the waterline in a low crouch, watching the jungle as best I could until I'd reached a cluster of boulders in the shallow water.

Sliding behind them, I leaned back against the nearest one until I'd caught my breath. My hand was covered in blood, so I bent down and dipped it in the ocean. The water was cool but not cold. It washed me clean. The blood coiled and drifted away on the tide, turning and twisting like the living thing it was.

I peered around the side of the rocks. But for the three bodies farther down the beach, the sand was empty. I snuck out, keeping low, and hurried between the boulders, across a small section of sand and into the jungle, continuing on despite having no idea where I was headed. Ignoring the branches and leaves tearing at me as I went, I increased speed, running harder and deeper into the lush foliage, bloody visions exploding through my shredded mind as I went.

After several minutes I emerged from the thick jungle and found myself on the side of a hill, a large area of grassy land before me with a forest beyond. There seemed no sign of human life here, no hint that this land was tamed or inhabited by anyone.

But there were others, and they were near. I could feel them.

I could also feel Shadow. He was watching me.

Dropping down, I spun and slowly took in the panorama. The incessant brightness made it difficult to see any great distance, and everything here was green and distracting. Blinking and rubbing at my eyes, I managed to gain my bearings, then tried to determine which direction Shadow would come from.

If he had traversed the side of the cliffs and then cut directly into the jungle, as I suspected, he was likely either behind me or to my left. Either way, he'd still be in the jungle and not yet to the grassy hills. The others had likely continued on in the direction I was now facing, though I saw no trace of them. Still, the grass beyond the slope where I was crouched was even higher—roughly to my waist—so it could've easily concealed them had they chosen to hide there.

I waited. I watched.

One of the jungle-dwellers appeared near the bottom of the slope. Standing slowly, he emerged from the grass. Facing the section of jungle to my left, he opened wide his arms, as if in welcome, then tilted his head back and stared at the sun.

An arrow appeared, suddenly, in his upper chest. He stood, unmoving, arms still out wide. Another missile struck an inch or so next to the first, and this time the man fell back, straight as a board, swallowed by the swaying grass.

The last two were up and running, exploding out of the grass and charging toward the jungle from which the arrows had come. Their brother had sacrificed himself to draw out the shooter, and fast and hard as they were running, I knew they'd never make it.

One was down seconds later, an arrow in his eye that left him spinning and wailing before dropping into the tall grass and going quiet. The second, and last of the band that had initially approached me, continued the charge, swinging a club over his head and releasing a primal scream even when Shadow stepped from the jungle to show himself.

I stood up, watched.

Still in his trench coat, Shadow carefully slung his bow around his shoulder and onto his back, then pulled a tomahawk from his belt and stood his ground, waiting for the man to reach him. When he did, he easily sidestepped him and brought the tomahawk around and down into the center of the man's back. As he fell, Shadow went with him, landing on his knees only to yank the blade free, then slam it down again, this time into the back of the man's skull.

After a moment, he stood up, wiped the blade on the side of

his coat, then slid the tomahawk back into his belt. He straightened his hat so the brim would shield the sun and better hide his dark eyes. Then he started toward me.

I stayed where I was, the ax held down by my side.

When he was within a few feet of me, he stopped. We stared at each other a while. Neither of us spoke. The wind picked up, blowing in off the nearby ocean and sending the tall grass swaying back and forth. Shadow was spattered with blood but didn't seem to mind. Like me, he'd been through an unimaginable ordeal to get here, and it showed, but he was still the same stone-cold killer he'd always been. He hadn't come through pristine, but nothing ever fazed Shadow. Nothing ever would.

"What do you think?" I finally said. "Is this the Promised Land?"

He didn't answer.

"Or are we in Hell?"

"Hell's dreams maybe," he said in his typical monotone.

"You didn't have to kill them."

Again, he gave no reply.

"They could've taken me to Julia."

"There is no Promised Land, Monk. There is no Hell." His long dark hair blew in the wind. "There might not even be a Julia."

"She's here."

"Don't matter."

"It's *all* that matters."

"She's just one more invisible, merciless god."

I wanted to say something like it didn't have to be this way or it didn't have to come to this, but we both knew that was a lie. This was exactly how it had to be. Neither of us was ever going back, and we both knew that too. Heaven or Hell, none of that mattered now; neither one had any use for our kind.

"Say your prayers to her then," he told me. "Tell her your sins."

I held the ax tight. "She is my sin."

Shadow slowly turned and looked out at the hills. I followed his gaze.

More jungle-dwellers, too many to count, dotted the landscape, standing in lines across the hills and in the flatland between us and them. All with the blood along their faces, all carrying weapons, they neither moved nor made a sound. It was as if they'd appeared out of thin air.

I looked behind us. Even more had formed a line along the edge of the jungle.

Shadow and I exchanged glances.

With a long sigh, he shrugged off his coat and let it fall to the ground along with his bow and quiver of arrows. With surprising care, he removed his hat, placed it atop his coat, then pulled back his hair and let it fall behind his shoulders. He noticed one particularly wet patch of blood on his shirt and dabbed his thumb in it. Without a word, he painted a cross with it that ran from his forehead down along the bridge of his nose. He then tore open his shirt, pulled it off and tossed it into the grass.

I wondered if the cross meant anything to him or if it was just a mark of war.

I wondered who his gods were, or if he had any.

Shadow looked at me and winked. With his tomahawk in one hand and large hunting knife in the other, he began a purposeful walk through the grass toward those along the edge of the hills and forest beyond.

I stayed where I was.

They killed him at the edge of the tall grass, beat him to death with their makeshift axes and clubs, stabbed him with their spears and knives, kicked and punched and beat him until he was dead.

But not before he'd taken out at least a dozen of them.

Then they came for me.

I would fight no more. If Julia was a prophet, then surely I was no longer a destroyer but instead a missionary, her disciple in this place of unimaginable wonder.

Tossing the ax away, I fell to my knees, closed my eyes, and just as Shadow had told me, prayed to my god and confessed to her my sins.

CHAPTER SIXTEEN

Julia was wrong. She'd always claimed we couldn't dream, not here, not now. But I did dream. Like before, I dreamed. I dreamed of this place. I dreamed of her.

Breaking through the edge of the jungle, she made her way toward me with a slow and languid gait, her hair draping her face, beautiful eyes bright but saddled with black bags, remnants of her journey, I suspected. Clad in a loincloth and bra made of animal skin, she looked as if she hadn't slept well in some time. She stopped short of me and smiled cautiously.

It broke what was left of my heart.

The others were there too, the jungle-dwellers, close and attentive.

"Julia," I said softly, wanting to be sure it was really her.

She opened her arms, and I closed the distance between us in a single step, crashing into her arms and taking her into mine as our cheeks met and I whispered to her how much I loved her, how much I'd missed her.

"I never thought I'd see you again," she said, her lips brushing my ear.

Her voice sounded different, deeper and raspier than normal, but I didn't care. All I wanted was to take hold of her and feel her against me.

"Did you really think I'd ever stop looking for you?"

Julia answered with a kiss. Her lips, chapped and dry, pressed hard against my own. We kissed with a passion and need that, until that moment, I hadn't been sure I'd ever know again. Her tongue slid into my mouth and met mine, and I held her tighter, my arms pressing her harder and harder against me.

"I'm sorry," she whispered a moment later. "But there was no other way."

We separated enough to look each other in the eye.

"You know that," she added, "don't you?"

In those beautiful and tired eyes, I saw truth.

"*Don't* you?"

"Yes." I ran a hand along the side of her face. "But how did you survive?"

"There were times I was sure I wouldn't. I traveled mostly in the light, and slept in darkness whenever I could. And then, the children."

"The ones who surround their village with heads on spikes…"

"We all do what we feel we must to survive."

"You lied to them."

"No."

"You won't be back for them. You're no fairy godmother."

"I'm strong, more powerful than you think. My magic always has been."

I couldn't argue with that, so I indicated the others with a slight nod of my head. "Runners?"

"Those that survived and made it this far, yes."

"What's wrong with them?"

"Why should there be anything wrong with them?"

"They way they look, the—the blood from their eyes, it—"

"The light. It *changes* you."

I thought of the inhabitants of Photas, the City of the Night Sleepers. Horrible, what the light had done to them. "We have to talk," I said. "Alone."

"They're just watching over me."

"You don't need protection from me."

"Are you sure?"

The question hurt but I understood why she needed to ask it. I nodded, held her face in my hands and kissed her again. Hand-in-hand, we strolled along the water's edge, moving slowly across the beach. "It's real," she said. "All of it."

"You know others are on their way to this place," I said quietly. "They're coming after me and you and everyone else here, and they won't stop until we're all terminated and this place is destroyed. You know that, don't you?"

"It doesn't matter," Julia said whimsically, as if she no longer had a care in the world. "Even if they survive the journey, it changes you."

"Not them."

"You'll see," she said, leaning into me and resting her head on my shoulder as we walked along the wet sand. "Everything's changed."

"We can never go back."

"Would you want to? Even if you could, would you want to?"

My head spinning, I tightened my grip on her as we left the sand and walked over an embankment, across a dune and down the other side. There, we found a patch of jungle. It was amazing, unlike anything I'd ever seen. The sounds and smells and sights—the animals—real, living animals not assigned to a dream or never seen unless as food, but alive and thriving—all of it an impossible fantasy come true right before my eyes.

Within minutes, we stepped out and into a peaceful lagoon encircled by more jungle. The beauty here was even more pronounced than the beach from which we'd come. More coconut palms swayed in the slow, warm breeze, exotic flowers and plants spotted the edges of the jungle, and the same white sand

and perfectly clear water glistened in the bright sunshine, the latter teeming with colorful fish unlike any I had ever seen. In the distance, deeper into the jungle, the sound of a waterfall echoed through the lagoon.

The others were still with us, tagging along from behind, and every now and then I'd hear them snickering or whispering amongst themselves. But my focus was on Julia. Despite how horrible her trek must have been, she seemed exhausted but unhurt. She bore no wounds except for a bruise or a scrape here or there, nothing significant or worrisome.

"Where are we going?" I asked.

Rather than answer, Julia smiled dreamily and led me into the heart of the lagoon, where the village these runners had made for themselves came into view.

A series of huts had been constructed twenty or so yards into the jungle, along with another larger building, all of them situated in a cleared open area. Perhaps fifty people in all, nearly every race and color was represented, and while there were a handful of older people, everyone else was young. A group of men walked by us, glancing at me with suspicion but general disinterest as they grabbed spears and headed out into the water, presumably to fish. Others were working at various chores, some boiling rice and other edibles in large pots, leaving me to wonder where these things came from or how they obtained them, while others still lounged about, some in handmade hammocks strung between trees and others lying out on the sandy beach.

"Doesn't seem possible this many could've made it."

"They've been lying to all of us, even you."

"So this is the Promised Land then?" I asked. "This is paradise?"

"Some think so," she said.

"But not you?"

Julia shook her head, traced the sand at our feet with her toe. "This is something in between. The Promised Land lies on the other side of the ocean."

"How do you know?"

"I was right about this, wasn't I?"

"Why don't they all go there then? Why do so many stay?"

She smiled. "Staying here doesn't require faith, only acceptance."

"What if there's nothing beyond the ocean?"

"You used to tell me there was no ocean."

"Why have *you* stayed then?"

"Maybe I was waiting for you." She slung an arm around my shoulder. "Or maybe I'm already gone."

"Am I dreaming?" I asked.

"Not yet, my love...not yet."

"So what happens then?"

"When?"

"When...if...we reach the Promised Land?"

Julia licked her lips and stared off into the jungle as if her answer resided there. "Life," she said, barely above a whisper. "Real life, do you understand? Then, and only then, will we dream. They'll be *our* servants, and *we'll* live in the light. And in those dreams, *our* dreams, we'll be free."

I watched as she broke away from me, stepped into the lagoon and pushed off, swimming deeper into the clear water. The others remained behind me, standing guard, and I felt their contempt. I knew what they wanted to do to me, and perhaps I deserved it. Who could say? Maybe none of us were ever truly forgiven for anything.

Maybe we shouldn't be.

Pain slams my skull.

Something tickled my eyebrow, and I felt it run along the side of my face. I knew it was blood, I didn't have to check, didn't have to run my fingers through it or even look. I stood there and let it flow.

Julia, on her back now, kicked and drifted deeper into the lagoon.

Are you all right?

I wanted to drop into the water too. I wanted to swim out

to where she was and join her, to put my arms around her and feel her wet skin against mine. But instead, my legs buckled and I fell to my knees as the blood flowed over my eyes, blinding me. A metallic taste ran across my lips, into my mouth, coated my tongue and throat.

Can you hear me?

Why was Julia still swimming, I wondered?

Everything begins to bend and move, and the pain grows even worse.

Why wasn't she with me, holding me, helping me, saving me?

Can you hear me?

I'd come so far, so goddamn far to find her, to rescue us both.

Nearby, I heard the waterfall splashing, but all I could think about was the city, with its darkness and rain and violence, and the cramped little apartment Julia and I had once called home. Me, a man of rules, procedure and death. She, a woman existing to inhabit the dreams and nightmares of others. And now we *were* the others.

Who inhabited our dreams then? Who haunted our nightmares?

I opened my eyes and saw the jungle-dwellers closing on me, running through the tall grass, their bloodstained weapons raised above their heads, ready to smash me to pieces as they had Shadow.

Like so much water running between my fingers and dripping from my hands, I couldn't hold on to Julia. She slipped away, across that lagoon and back into memory, the paradise replaced with a field of tall grass swaying in a warm ocean wind.

Savage cries of vengeance and cruelty swirled around me like blood in the water. The water in my dreams…

The sun turned bloody and red, then slowly black. Rotten. Diseased.

"What is the price?" I heard Julia ask, her breath hot and sensuous in my ear. "What is the price of our *addictions*, our dreams?"

Not darkness, but light.

CHAPTER SEVENTEEN

Sitting at a dressing table, clad in her flimsy nightgown, Julia looks back over her shoulder at me as the darkness grows stronger. Everything blurs and shakes.

"Are you all right?"

Canned laughter coming from a small black-and-white television in the corner absorbs the sound of her voice. Rabbit ear antennas sit atop the television, but the screen is filled with snow, the signal so distorted it's imperceptible. Odd sounds leak from the television along with the robotic laughter, barely human gibberish filtered through odd, rumbling, machine-like noises. Julia turns away, looks at me through the mirror over the dressing table. "Can you hear me?" she asks bitterly.

Everything begins to bend and move, and terrible pain fires through my skull.

The world liquefies, and with a thunderous roar, becomes something else.

"Can you hear me?" she asks, urgently this time. *"Can you hear me?"*

* * *

My body was limp and useless, but I could still raise my head enough to see beyond the bow of the small boat I found myself in. Unsure if I'd crawled onto it or had been placed here, I lay on my stomach in a pool of my own blood, bobbing along the waves. The darkness was almost complete, and a heavy fog wrapped everything else in its mystery. I coughed, tasted blood and bile, blinked the same from my eyes, and squinted into the semi-darkness ahead. Was there something there, or just more night and ocean?

In the silence of sorrow, I am a forgotten and soulless old man, sitting in my chair, my legs covered with a blanket. I cannot breathe as I should, as I need to, and as I fall away from that little white room I thought so safe, away from Julia and her dressing table and her flimsy nightgown, the symbols and signs are everywhere, flooding back into my mind in a violent rush of madness. And concealed in all this lunacy are the tricks that make me numb to the night, at least for a time, and protect me from the dark, deadly and depraved streets of my home.

Despite horrific pain, I managed to pull an arm free from beneath me. Reaching for the darkness ahead with broken fingers slick with blood, I tried to touch the form I was so certain I could see wrapped in the slowly drifting mist and fog. Julia, standing on nearby land, or perhaps floating above the ocean waves like the dispossessed deity she'd become.

"Have you ever listened to the stories about the world of light?" she asked, her voice ghostly and distant. "I mean *really* listened."

I tried to touch her, to extend my arm far enough into the fog to feel her with my fingertips, but she was too far away, grinning at me now as if insane.

She just kept laughing.

"Help me," I gasped, as the pain in my face and head grew worse, and blood erupted from my lips in a thick crimson spray. "Help me…"

Like a madwoman.

The fog engulfed her, swallowed her whole, and slowly became a rain of blood. My blood, flying and bursting from me with each swing of their horrible clubs, each stab and slash of their spears. These were not waves, but slowly swaying stalks of grass.

Amidst nearly unimaginable pain and violence, my eyes rolled to white as I felt the last remnants of a dying sun pulse against my bloodied face.

If we knew the sun, do you think we'd miss it?

Yes.

From the alleged safety of my chair, I look into Julia's eyes. The sadness in her face is gone, and this time, as she sits at her dressing table, she smiles as if she hasn't a care in the world.

"Are you all right?" she asks.

I think of my mother, Gideon, who is not really my mother, in her abandoned library, and wish for a moment I could throw off this blanket and go to her, rest my head on her shoulder and feel her arms around me as she tells me everything will be all right.

I think of Julia's mother, Lenore, who is not really her mother, surrounded by her depravity and dead flies, and wish I could go to her and tell her it's not her fault, that she never had any choice.

None of us do.

I think of my childhood, which was never truly my own, and my puppy, and how I loved him. How I would give anything to feel his cold wet nose against my face just one more time, and forget all about what was waiting for me beyond those memories.

But these are the dreams of a much younger man. My dreams betray me, as they betray us all, drifting up from the filthy gutters and rain-soaked, darkened alleys, searching for the light, the sun, that which is warm and comforting and safe and certain and clean. Even though the light does horrible things to those in the dark, because truth is its weapon, and it is lethal.

I tried to speak, but couldn't. They'd taken that from me, just as they'd taken what life I had left. Whatever remained was slipping from me now, sneaking away like a thief. But in my mind, I could still see Julia in that slowly rolling fog, so beautiful there, just beyond my reach...

I whispered to her in my mind, and she smiled at me the way no one else ever could. I knew then that she could hear me.

If I never know peace, if I never again feel the touch of your hand, the warmth of your breath or the weight of your body against mine, let me know at least that we existed in each other, that we lived and remembered and are remembered, just as we remember every bit of laughter, every sigh, every moment of joy and agony, every tear, every breath drawn, every drop of blood spilled, every kiss. Let us know and remember these things, and realize that in this world, if only for a moment, we mattered.

If you ask me how it all ended, I won't answer. Not because I don't want to but because I don't know. Do any of us? Not really. Not totally. All I knew for sure was Julia had gone missing, and me with her, into the night, the darkness, the dreams and nightmares of the living and the dead, the awake and the sleeping. Maybe we were both on that same boat, riding the waves across an enormous ocean, and as the bow pierced the fog before us, we held each other and waited for what lay on the other side.

Old William, up to his old deviltry again...

Maybe I was lying in that tall grass, thinking of her as I bled to death.

I closed my eyes, perhaps in sleep.

Death's counterfeit...

Or maybe I was right back in that rainy old city.

All those godforsaken souls...

Maybe I'd never left. Maybe I never could.

Darkness is a cage, child.

"Can you hear me?"

Light is that cage door swung open wide.

"Can you hear me?"

"Don't fear the tempest, my love," I said. "These are our dreams, our addictions."

"Are you all right?"

"And in them, I am yours, and you are mine."

Far from all the violence and darkness, horror and blood, and bathed instead in the warmth of a sun we could never know, I pulled Julia close and we kissed, gently and as if forever, our dreams now one.

On the dark and lonely streets of Babylon.

Greg F. Gifune is a best-selling, internationally-published author of several acclaimed novels, novellas, and two short story collections. Working predominantly in the horror and crime genres, Greg has been called "the best writer of horror and thrillers at work today" by *New York Times* best-selling author Christopher Rice, "one of the best writers of his generation" by both *The Roswell Literary Review* and horror grandmaster Brian Keene, and "among the finest dark suspense writers of our time" by legendary best-selling author Ed Gorman. Greg's work has been published all over the world, translated into several languages, received starred reviews from *Publishers Weekly, Library Journal, Kirkus* and others, is consistently praised by readers and critics alike, and has garnered attention from Hollywood. Two of his short stories, "Hoax" and "First Impressions," have been adapted to film. His novel, *Children of Chaos*, is currently under a development deal to be made into a television series.

His novel, *The Bleeding Season*, originally published in 2003, has been hailed as a classic in the horror genre and is considered to be one of the best horror/thriller novels of the decade.

Greg resides in Massachusetts with his wife, Carol, a few cats, and a dog named Dozer. He can be reached online at gfgauthor@verizon.net or on Facebook and Twitter.